Tony looked haggard, as if he hadn't slept since the cruise. "You don't know how I've felt, knowing I might lose you all over again once you knew the truth," he continued.

"You never had me to lose. You agreed it was just going to be sex and you would walk away!" How could Emma be so angry that he hadn't really walked out of her life when just moments ago she'd been cursing herself for letting him do just that? How could she want to throw herself into his arms and strangle him at the same time?

"I knew I'd have to see you again," he said simply. "But I wanted you to have your fantasy first."

She smiled grimly. "Yes, you were my fantasy, all right...." She wrapped her arms around her waist. "I don't even know you."

"Oh, I think we got to know each other rather intimately," he said, cupping her chin in his hand. "I know that your eyes go all hazy when you get aroused, and I know the way you like to be stroked along your beautiful back. I know that you're ticklish behind your knees and that you sigh in your sleep."

He tilted her face so that she looked him in the eye. "And I think we *both* know that this fantasy *isn't* over...."

Blaze™

Dear Reader,

When I won the *Romantic Times BOOKclub* Reviewers Choice Award for Best First Series Romance for 2004, I was writing for Harlequin Temptation. Then I was told that I would be writing my first book for Harlequin Blaze, and I was so intrigued. It couldn't have come at a more remarkable time in my life——I'm single again. So Emma's cruise into sexual experimentation might be based on my own voyage of sexual discovery. Of course, in the old days a lady never told, but today a lady not only tells, she goes for it!

I hope you enjoy discovering Emma's sexual exploits with her Bahama boy toy. And I hope you'll be excited to know that her best friend, Tina, is getting her own book. Because being a sexual mentor and sidekick just didn't do this girl justice. She's got a stripper in her *wrong* bed and what she does with him will heat up your sheets! Be sure to read it in bed, preferably with someone to strip down for you!

I hope you enjoy reading about these very different but enticing women stepping up to the challenge of finding a man who gives them all the pleasure they've dreamed about. Enjoy the adventure!

Sincerely,

Mara Fox

LETTING GO!

Mara Fox

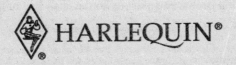

HARLEQUIN®

TORONTO • NEW YORK • LONDON
AMSTERDAM • PARIS • SYDNEY • HAMBURG
STOCKHOLM • ATHENS • TOKYO • MILAN • MADRID
PRAGUE • WARSAW • BUDAPEST • AUCKLAND

ISBN 0-373-79261-1

LETTING GO!

Copyright © 2006 by Mara Fox Horstman.

This edition published by arrangement with Harlequin Books S.A.

® and TM are trademarks of the publisher. Trademarks indicated with
® are registered in the United States Patent and Trademark Office, the
Canadian Trade Marks Office and in other countries.

www.eHarlequin.com

Printed in U.S.A.

ABOUT THE AUTHOR

After wandering the county as a military brat, author Mara Fox was happy to settle in a little Texas town with the friendliest people she'd ever met and the biggest sky she'd ever seen. And she thought it was like catching hold of one of those stars when she won the *Romantic Times BOOKclub* Reviewers Choice Award for Best First Series Romance for 2004. These days she's going to college and spreading her single wings, both figuratively and not so figuratively. Turns out that Emma and Mara have a lot in common! There might even be a singles cruise to the Bahamas in the works....

Books by Mara Fox

HARLEQUIN TEMPTATION

982—I SHOCKED THE SHERIFF

I'm happy to dedicate this book to Brenda Chin, the best editor, mentor and friend anyone could have in her corner, especially in a tight spot.

Prologue

GAZING THROUGH the glass at Emma, Anthony Enderlin wondered if this would be a good time to introduce himself to the woman who had lured him to the law firm of Anderson-Harding with her siren voice.

Though he felt they knew each other, they'd never actually met. They'd only spoken. And her voice had teased, cajoled and flirted with him, affecting him the way he imagined good phone sex might. It had stayed with him, sneaking into the most unexpected corners of his life.

And they'd only talked a couple of times while co-ordinating a work program.

It was damn disconcerting.

So he'd decided to come and do the computer installation himself. It would surely get her out of his system, so to speak. He'd sold the idea to his boss as a field test of sorts and vacation. Now he was spinning his wheels...lurking.

He heard footsteps in the hall. Emma's best friend, the lady lawyer they called The Shark, was approaching, and feeling guilty, he stepped back as though he hadn't been hanging around outside the employee break room like a moonstruck idiot.

He ran his hand through his hair and sighed. Turning, he headed towards the office where yet another lawyer would expect him to debug a computer constipated with porn, viruses and fragments of old games.

Which was a huge waste of his expertise.

After all, he was the designer of the software, and he'd coordinated the project with Emma, the company's liaison. When he'd come to do the install, he hadn't planned on spending his time cleaning up each and every lawyer's computer system.

He'd hoped to do a bit more *liaisoning.*

With Emma.

Because that voice had flowed over him like silk and sex.

Tony had known that Emma couldn't possibly look as good as she sounded. He knew he'd get over the infatuation when they finally met. Then they'd become friends because talking to Emma made him feel good. Besides, he was better at friendship than dating. For some reason, no matter how attractive the woman he was dating, one of his programs usually wooed him and the woman walked away.

What he needed was a woman who could seduce him from his cyber world.

The Shark walked by in sharp, echoing heels. He avoided eye contact by pretending to be reading the printout in his hand. Not that she'd know him. He'd managed to avoid her so far.

She was striking in a sleek way, but Emma's softer beauty was even more attractive. Once he'd seen Emma, he'd had difficulty imagining her as just a friend. She looked like a character who had just stepped out of a Camelot novel. Or out of one of the role-playing games he preferred when he got tired of programming. He enjoyed adventures with knights, dragons, quests and swordplay.

He spent a lot of time rescuing the princess.

However, this princess had enough gumption to rescue herself, and he knew from their conversations that she was also a smart, funny, sexy woman, even if right now she was hiding out in the break room after a bad breakup.

So she was a bit self-conscious, too. Interesting.

It was a fascinating contradiction that Tony planned to examine closer. He no longer saw Emma becoming a friend, he wanted more. But he didn't know how much more. They lived half a country apart. And he wasn't a player—he spent too much time in front of a computer screen to be able to brag about his dating exploits. Then there was his short attention span.

So the "liaisoning" would be short-term. Better everyone understood that up front.

He could be charming, his sister had told him. And according to the office gossip, Emma had just gotten burned by a first-class jerk, so she might go for a gentleman.

They might have some laughs together.

He might get to listen to that silken voice at a much closer proximity. Whispering love words in his ear.

He smiled at his little fantasy.

So much for thinking like a gentleman.

So far he hadn't even managed to meet her or shake

her hand. Instead he was stuck purging computers. Making himself useful so the boss didn't send him home.

It made his fingers itch. The longer she hid out, the more determined he was to uncover everything about Emma…

1

EMMA DANIELS sat in the break room looking gloomily at her sprouts-and-avocado sandwich. Beside the sandwich sat a supersize bar of white chocolate which she determinedly ignored.

I deserve this candy bar for holding my head up, but if I eat candy then I won't be able to get into my skinny clothes so I can start the whole dating thing again.

Dating.

She sank lower in her seat, sighing at the dismal thought.

Since it was after two o'clock in the afternoon, she had the break room to herself, until her friend Tina Henderson breezed in looking like a million bucks in her green Gucci suit. Emma sat up straighter in her chair.

"Are you still mooning over that chocolate bar?"

"It's a different one. I'm eating a new kind everyday."

"You're lying through those pearly whites. Have you been using whitening stripes again?"

Emma looked up. "I'm preparing for the most grueling ritual of our time—dating. That thing you do so effortlessly, like managing to look fresh in this

humidity. My stupid hair's frizzing all over the place."
She tugged self-consciously on her braid; it had been
raining in Jacksonville, Florida, all month long.

"How can your hair curl? You're wearing that French
braid so tight my head aches in sympathy."

Emma grimaced. "I'm thinking of getting it professionally straightened. How'd the case go?"

"Great. Easy. We won. When are you going to quit
fooling around as a paper pusher and go back to school?
I need someone sharp to be my paralegal. I need you."
Tina opened the fridge.

"I missed the deadline for night school again."

"Why? I thought you were serious this time."

"I am. But Melissa needed me. We're getting everyone ready for the installation of the new computer program. It's supposed to save all kinds of time and money
and she begged me and then she bribed me with heavy
overtime and used her I-know-what's-best-for-you
voice. The upside is I managed to pay off my credit
cards. The downside is I was so busy I didn't realize the
deadline had come and gone." Emma stuck out one foot,
clad in a Jimmy Choo shoe. "I ended up shopping just
to console myself. But next semester's deadline is on my
calendar in red ink and I'm not going to miss it no
matter who needs me. This time I'm going to make sure
I do something for *myself.*"

Thinking about her future security made her
thoughts stray to her father's midlife crisis. "You can
only rely on yourself, and I'm not going to allow
anyone else to sidetrack me this time," she said
hesitantly.

"That's an excellent observation but I'm still afraid I'll be retiring before you get around to it."

Emma grimaced. "Part of the problem is that I like being secretary to a partner. It's interesting and challenging. I just wish there was a little more respect and money to go along with the title."

"Everyone in the office respects you."

Emma shook her head. "Not everyone. School is definitely the way to go. Speaking of paralegals, did you hire Lee Matheson?"

"I should. He's hot." Tina shot her a look. "Did you know he's engaged?"

Emma swung her foot in frustration; at least it looked good in her new shoes. "I know. While I was thinking about calling him, someone else snagged him. It's like I'm the queen of hesitation. While I'm burning time calculating the pros and cons of a situation, I miss out. But I'm working on it."

Tina made a sympathetic noise and then poked around inside the fridge. "What's in here that belongs to you? I'm starving and I'm ready to mooch. Why are you eating so late anyway? Is Melissa looking down her nose at you over those granny glasses, guilting you into working harder? And they call me The Shark," Tina said with obvious satisfaction.

"No, she's in court today. I just didn't feel very hungry." Emma pushed her sandwich towards the other side of the table. "Here, you can eat the avocado and sprouts. I've got three rice bowls in the freezer for emergencies."

"You're a lifesaver," Tina said reverently.

Emma got up to look in the freezer. She certainly was no shark, just a wuss, but she planned to work on it.

Tina pounced on the sandwich. "I sure could have used you today in court when the defendant got so nervous she spilled water all over my notes. You would have had the notes copied in triplicate."

I'm definitely the queen of triplicate.

Emma examined the generic chicken-and-rice picture on one of the rice bowls. Being cautious was supposed to keep her life from becoming chaotic, but it had become mind-numbing.

"Hey, Emma, what's wrong? You're scowling at a rice bowl."

Emma shoved the rice bowl back into the freezer and turned to face her successful friend. "I just feel left behind. I passed on Lee that day he flirted with me because I was waffling, and then I ended up with Brad."

"I thought you might be hiding out here because of Brad."

Emma refused to shed the tears clogging her throat. "He embarrassed the hell out of me."

"Yes, I know he did." Tina put the sandwich down again. "He got fired. That should make you feel a little better."

"He got caught in the copy room with Angela. How could he care so little about me that he'd grope a woman's breasts at the place where we both work? And that's after he gave me the lecture about how I'm settling for a job that's beneath me. Obviously, nothing's beneath him—though I suppose Angela was." She sighed.

"Everyone knows who gets things done around here.

Brad's just an idiot. He didn't really care about your job title or he wouldn't have gone after a clerk."

Emma looked down at her chest. "A double-D clerk."

Tina smiled. "On your frame, double-D's would look ridiculous. Besides, Angela's are fake."

Emma leaned forward. "Seriously?"

"Yeah, she almost got fired for taking such a long leave after the surgery. Essentially, Brad was groping silicone."

Emma almost chuckled. "Did he have to do it here? I can't even come in here during the lunch hour for all of the sympathetic glances. It drives me crazy. The only good thing is that I don't have to see them for a few days. They're getting trained on the new system this week. I'm just following up, making sure everyone's completed the course and I can do most of it by e-mail."

"What happened to the personal touch? Everyone's concerned because you're hiding in your office."

Emma shrugged.

"You're making too big a deal out of this."

"Am I?" She shook her head. "Why didn't Brad just insist we have sex? I wanted sex, just not right away. I thought I should have a few dates to get to know each other before we jumped into a physical relationship."

Tina humphed. "You didn't have sex with Brad because there wasn't any chemistry. A part of you recognized he was a loser."

"Maybe." Emma shrugged. "So I'm back to dating. And it sucks big-time. Either I hesitate and the guy turns out to be a great guy, or I jump in and the guy's a loser. I always seem to get my heart broken or my pride stepped on. Why do we do this? It's like a series of bad job interviews with sex." She jiggled her leg again, "Maybe I should get my belly button pierced or a tattoo."

Tina smirked. "You're too practical for a navel ring. A little tattoo might be okay but you should get something like that to make a statement. It should mean something. I hate it when some guy just gets one because he's under the influence of alcohol and a bunch of idiots convinced him to put his girlfriend's name on his neck."

Emma couldn't help but grin. "Only you would think a tattoo was a rite of passage. And why do we bother with men anyway?"

Emma couldn't admit to Tina she had always wanted a tattoo and hadn't yet had the guts to get one.

"We bother with dating because men have better anatomical equipment than we can buy on the Internet."

"That's pretty crude, girlfriend." Emma smirked.

"How long has it been since you've challenged yourself when it came to men? Really gone for it when it came to romance?"

"Since the word *romance* isn't usually part of your vocabulary, let me guess what you really mean. This must be about the singles' cruise to the Bahamas."

Tina picked at the sprouts on her plate. "Darcy bugged out on me. I desperately need a roommate. I just put a huge down payment on my new condo, so I could really use the group discount they're offering."

"You've already talked some of the staff into going. And I don't know about a singles' cruise. It sounds kinda desperate."

"Lighten up. It'll be fun."

"You can't think *you* need to go on a singles' cruise."

"Just think of it as a love boat. I'm going because it's a chance to relax and enjoy the company of single men. Dating takes too much time away from court." She stretched out her arms. "I'm looking forward to *hot* summer nights and *sultry* summer days."

Emma smiled. "You mean hot, sultry sex. But I've heard their cruises really do rock."

"Come and find out for yourself."

"You don't need me."

Tina took a sip of water. "Yes I do. There's no one going that I'd want to share a bathroom with."

"How can you have a fling, with me in your room? I might cramp your style."

"Don't worry. I'll manage a fling with or without a roommate. I'll show you how it's done. Come on. It'll be fun."

Emma hesitated. "Having a fling on a cruise sounds so…dangerous."

"Couldn't get much worse than Brad."

"That's not fair."

"Are you looking for something long-term? Do you think that's safer? Have you looked at the divorce statistics? I know a couple of lawyers who specialize in divorce and they make a lot more money than I do."

Emma pulled the corner of the candy-bar wrapper open. "Considering that my parents got divorced after twenty-five years of marriage, you have a valid point."

"Go on the cruise with me, score a little romance, practice safe sex while you're going for the gusto, and learn how to scuba or snorkel or Jet Ski even. It'll be an adventure. Then, when you come back, everyone will be talking about you instead of your ex." Tina winked.

Emma *could* imagine a little romance on a moonlit beach. It felt like a decade since she'd had sex. Could she leave the wussy behind and be a pussy-cat? She smiled at her own audacity. Tina would have been proud if Emma could have said it without blushing.

Why do I have to second-guess everything, anyway?

Even the thought of the cruise had her thinking differently. "Maybe if I were more spontaneous my life would be more interesting," she said tentatively.

"Honey, when you run into the right man it'll be more than interesting—it'll be sizzling."

"On the cruise I won't have to look for anything further in a man than a nice tan and a great body—since I'm not taking him home or anything." Emma pulled more of the wrapper off the candy and then she set it down again. "I wouldn't even have to consider a future with a man I'm never going to see again. I could concentrate on living in the moment."

"That's my girl."

She nodded decisively. "Let's use the computer in my office to sign me up for the cruise. I think a moonlit beach and a gorgeous playboy might be just the thing. I could really go for it."

"Just so long as *it* is covered with a condom."

"I'm going to do anything and everything on this cruise."

Tina laughed. "Down, girl. Be gentle."

Emma smiled to herself as she got up to choose a rice

bowl. She reached into the freezer looking for the chicken in spicy peanut sauce she'd grabbed by mistake in the grocery store. She ripped the wrapper before she could change her mind.

"You know," she told Tina as she thrust the bowl into the microwave and then headed toward the table to scoop up the chocolate "I think I might have developed an appetite after all." Emma bit into the delicious white chocolate with a smile of pure ecstasy. "I don't know what I've been waiting for. From now on I'm going to be eating my dessert first."

TONY ENDERLIN looked around the tiny stateroom with trepidation. "Why did I think this would be okay?" he asked himself aloud, fighting a severe case of claustrophobia. "I shouldn't be here."

In all fairness the cabin wasn't tiny and the ceiling was high enough for his six-foot frame to clear with room to spare, but it was the illusion of smallness that had him breathing hard. The way the doors sealed made him feel as if there wasn't enough air in the room.

Once, when he'd been six years old, he'd followed his cousin into one of those big, silver drainage pipes and then his cousin had hidden from him. In his hysteria Tony had actually run the wrong way, into a smaller pipe, where he'd tripped over the carcass of a long-dead animal and then slid into a puddle of rank water.

Small debris had fallen down on him every time he'd tried to get to his feet so he'd huddled in the dark with his imagination on *Fast Forward* while his body was firmly on *Pause*. That had been the longest twenty minutes of Tony's life. He'd been unable to move, even when his cousin had finally located him. That panic always crept back to choke him in closed-in areas, despite his best attempts to control his weakness.

That was one of the reasons he'd chosen Denver to call home; he'd never feel claustrophobic on a mountain. He threw himself down on the bed, rolled over on his back, and closed his eyes, pretending he was out on the deck with the endless blue sky above him. Slowly, his breathing smoothed out.

See how easy it is to stay in control? he told himself.

Except this cruise had really thrown him off.

One of the guys from the office had booked the private room on the cruise ship after a big fight with his girlfriend, and then they'd made up and eloped the very next day. As a married man, the guy couldn't very well go on a singles' cruise unless he wanted a divorce, so he'd offered Tony the opportunity to go on the cruise.

Aw, tell the truth. You're here because Emma Daniels is here.

It seemed she'd been persuaded to go on the singles' cruise to recuperate from her embarrassing boyfriend fiasco, and then the ticket had become available for him to use. Tony's Mexican grandmother, who'd given him his middle name of Andres, would praise the saints and call it fate, in fluent Spanish.

Tony called it opportunity. And he could have done so in fluent Spanish if he was so inclined.

Could a woman really be worth all of this trouble?

Oh yeah. Emma had a quick mind and a wicked

sense of humor. And that body. Who would have known the siren would have a body to match the sultry voice?

Since he'd been on site in Jacksonville, he'd only seen her through the window or from down the hall. Her dark blond hair always seemed to be trying to curl out of the braid thing she wore. It actually looked kinda nice, like a crown or something. Maybe that was why he thought she looked like a princess. But he didn't want to rescue her. He just wondered how her hair might look spread out and curling on a pillow.

Her height seemed average and her weight was just right, curvy in all the right places. Her eyes were blue. Or so he believed. Tony hadn't gotten nearly close enough to see her eyes and not for a lack of trying.

Fate or opportunity?

It didn't matter what you called it. He planned to get to know Emma Daniels. She'd looked so vulnerable sitting in the break room in the middle of the afternoon. And Tony hadn't found the opportunity to talk to her in person, though her witty e-mails had kept him going and she'd called his cell phone over concerns for the new software. Anderson-Harding was a big place and he'd seen it all except for the one person he wanted to meet.

He grinned, thinking of one particular lawyer who'd used up all of his RAM downloading porn, some of which had actually made Tony uncomfortable. Especially since one of the blondes on the screen had looked enough like Emma to spark all kinds of thoughts he'd be better off not thinking. He'd obviously been devoting too much time developing his new program.

Perhaps that was why Emma had made such an impression on him—too many long hours at the computer with only her voice on the phone to lure him away from the keyboard. He'd looked forward to their conversations, even when they were discussing the most casual topics. Her satiny-smooth voice had curled around him. The husky laugh had stimulated his imagination.

So when he'd picked up and traveled to Florida from Denver, it wasn't for the beaches. He'd needed to put a face to the voice that haunted his dreams.

This is silly. She's just a woman. Not a siren. Or medieval princess. It's my imagination that's my enemy. Emma's just a regular girl who will bore me to distraction after a couple of dates. Then I'll welcome getting back to my latest computer program.

Right now he couldn't concentrate. He couldn't work. He didn't like unsolved puzzles and his reaction to Emma was a puzzle. A puzzle he intended to take apart piece by piece until the enchantment went away.

I'll never know if I stay here feeling like the ceiling's coming down on my head.

Impatient with wasting his time and eager to begin his vacation and his quest, Tony climbed off the bunk, wincing only a little at his head's close proximity to the ceiling.

He went over to his duffel bag and reached inside for his swimsuit. Time to relax in a lounge chair by the pool and have a drink. Out where the sky was the limit and fate could take a leap.

Tony fully intended to enjoy his vacation. Maybe he'd pretend he was a player. He could do it. Warming to the idea, he smiled to himself. He'd play the hell outta the women on the cruise. After all, they expected to be *romanced*. It would be fun, like living in one of his role-playing games. And it would be smart to spread himself around, rather than spend all his time focused on Emma, a woman who couldn't possibly live up to what he'd built her up to be. He might even have a go at the slick lady lawyer.

TINA STEPPED over the lip of the doorway leading into the cabin. She noted that the bunks looked comfortable tucked against the wall and there was more floor space than she'd anticipated. The balcony door was covered by a colorful curtain. "I just love having a cabin with a balcony. It feels so luxurious," she announced.

Emma didn't look up from unpacking her suitcases. "The balcony's great. I just hope I won't be spending the entire cruise out there staring at the water because I'm too chicken to mingle with the men. All week I've been a nervous wreck anticipating this cruise."

"You won't have any trouble. Why are you unpacking so diligently? I left my luggage with a handsome young man—Italian, I think, although his English was gorgeous."

Emma finally looked up from where she'd been sorting the clothing. "I can't find anything—"

"Oh wow! What have you done to your hair?"

Emma reached up to touch the straight hair just brushing the tops of her shoulders. "I got it cut and high-lighted. Then the hairdresser sold me some expensive mousse that actually tames the frizz. It's your fault. You kept telling me that French braids were definitely out."

Tina took the few steps separating them in the small

cabin, tossed her bag on her bunk, then fluffed Emma's hair with her fingers. "It looks fabulous. Kind of 'rock star' and 'waif' at the same time. Maybe I should go back to being a blonde." She patted her own hair into place.

"I love yours. Every time it's different and yet just right. How do you do that?"

"I pay a hairdresser outrageously to know what to do. All I care about is that it changes once in a while. I don't like to be bored. In fact I don't remember exactly what my natural color is," she teased her friend.

"Why can't I be more adventurous like you?" Emma mused.

"Because you're so perfect at being Emma. Why would you want to be me? Your problem is that you don't see yourself very clearly."

"What do you mean?"

"Well, you've got all the basic equipment to be gorgeous, interesting and seductive but you don't always follow through."

"I'm not sure I know how."

"Why let idiots like Brad define you? Gorgeous is just making the most of your assets. Oh, that reminds me…" Tina walked over to the bed and rifled through Emma's suitcase until she came across a one-piece bathing suit, which she ceremoniously dropped in the trash can beside the desk in the compact cabin. "And I do mean *ass*ets. You'll need to buy a thong in the ship's store."

"A thong? I couldn't wear a thong!"

"Why not?" Tina patted Emma on the butt. "Honey, you've got the ass. Just get used to showing it off."

"I brought a skinny little black dress like you told me." Emma gazed longingly at the trash can.

"That's good. A little black dress is a must. And I brought some amazing makeup. The new you will be a striking, mysterious creature who doesn't tell all of the truth but just enough to be interesting."

"I'm not very good at lying." Her voice rose. "Why do I have to lie?"

"Why not? You're never going to see any of these men again. Anyway, I didn't say to lie. I just said to make the truth more interesting. You can even tell him something so true you've never told anyone else. Be daring. You're playing a game. The men on a singles' cruise expect you to play games and they really want to play along."

Emma seemed to be mulling that over; she tapped her chin with her forefinger as she usually did when she was thinking. The girl was brilliant. And pretty. And she didn't have a catty bone in her body. That was why she and Tina were such good friends. Emma had confidence where it counted, she didn't see Tina as a threat, as most women did. She just saw her as a friend.

"Hey, are you in there?" Tina prodded as she bent down to retrieve her overnight case.

Sinking down on the empty bunk, Emma said, "It was so amazing standing outside on the dock beside the huge ship, knowing I was the one going aboard. All kinds of possibilities seemed to be beckoning me. When they sounded a horn somewhere on the dock, it actually gave me a shiver."

"That's right. It'll be an adventure, if I can only find my...oh, I found it." Tina gestured triumphantly with a traffic-stopping red thong that she'd pulled out of her overnight bag. "What do you think? Is it seductive?"

"Is it legal in these waters?

"I hope not."

"It has occurred to me that I might be boarding the *Titanic*."

"What are you talking about?"

Emma ran her hand over one of the flowers on the tropical-print bedspread. "The seduction thing—everything—this might backfire big-time. I might be miserable."

Somehow Tina had to help Emma get back her confidence. So she took a chance. "Could it get any worse than the thing with Brad?"

Emma grimaced.

Tina shot the thong bottom across the room like a rubber band.

Emma ducked. She almost smiled. "I can't imagine how," she admitted.

"Then you've survived your version of the *Titanic* and now you're moving on. This hypothetical guy we speak of will never see you again. So it's up to you whether you cut him loose before or after you go back to your cabin. Seductive is just being open to the possibility of sex. It's a state of mind. And when you're trolling, men can feel your vibes. Let them drool all over you, dance with you, romance you, but remember, you're in charge. Don't choke. Enjoy it."

"I've never thought of it that way."

Tina smiled. "You think too much. This time just feel your way." She ran her hands down the curve of her waist.

Emma's face lit up and Tina wished her friend could

see herself when she was animated. Those ocean-blue eyes sparkled and she had a killer smile. "The men on this cruise aren't gonna know what hit them," Tina said with satisfaction.

"I'll bet I could get a thong bathing suit in the ship's store." Emma picked up the suit bottom and shot it back at Tina. "I'll bet I could get just about anything a girl could want on a singles' cruise to paradise."

"And we'll get a tattoo, a henna one to celebrate our adventure."

"That would be cool."

"But you have to have the adventure first. Remember you're going to be eating dessert first. And on a cruise you can order as many desserts as you like—tall, dark and handsome for the first course, athletic, tanned and blonde for the second and a Latin lover to go with your coffee."

"And everything's included in the original price so I can pig out without any guilt."

"Especially since what you have in mind won't be fattening. You'll be working it off." Tina winked.

Emma's grin stretched across her face.

Tina knew the only thing holding Emma back was her lack of confidence in how men perceived her. Maybe it had to do with her classic look, that girl-next-door phenomenon. Emma had no idea how much the new haircut did to get rid of that pesky image. Get her into a thong and the men would come running. Emma was going to get her chance and Tina was going to enjoy watching the show.

As they unpacked and discussed what Emma needed

from the ship's store, they were called away to participate in the ship-wide emergency drill.

Emma thought that everyone, including the usually
sophisticated Tina, looked silly in the bright yellow life
jackets, trooping up on deck to stand in line beside their
assigned lifeboats. Afterwards, Tina and Emma went to
the ship's store, which was packed with baubles, and
people, from all over the world.

Emma barely noticed when the ship left port
because she was trying on a pretty pair of thong underwear, which cost a considerable amount considering
how little it covered. And then, tugging self-consciously at the emerald-green-and-gold bathing suit
that had caught her eye, she finally let Tina peek in the
dressing room. "I don't think I have the figure for this
suit."

"Oh yes you do." Tina nodded decisively.

A few hundred dollars later Emma had a vacation
wardrobe consisting of two thong bikinis, two pretty
wraps to go over the revealing thongs and an extra little
black dress, even tinier than the one she already had.
And three pairs of thong underwear.

"It's a thong thing." Emma joked as she pulled out
her credit card. "I love the underwear but I can't believe
I'm going to wear the bikini in public."

"Fewer tan lines. Just think of it as exceedingly practical." Tina stood in line behind Emma with another
thong bikini and a sundress.

Hungry from the shopping spree, they grabbed a
quick lunch at a restaurant that boasted a huge salad bar,
and then took their food out on the deck.

"Look at that endless horizon. And we sure are speeding along. Amazing that we'll be in the Bahamas before dinner."

"It's not that far from Florida," Tina responded pragmatically.

"It's a different world. Out here on the ocean it feels like the sky's the limit. And anything else is just a restriction we put upon ourselves." Emma waved her fork at the view from the railing of the ship.

"True. But speaking philosophically—" Tina turned away from the view of the ocean to look at the men spread out on lounge chairs across the deck "—I prefer the old adage, so many men, so little time."

"Seven days ought to be enough time to work through a few of them," Emma said with a giggle.

Tina sat back. "Yes, a whole week to enjoy mindless, commitment-free release. No legal briefs, no clingy clients. Let even a hint of something real-life interfere with my vacation and I'll be running in the other direction."

Emma laughed.

"Anyway, I don't believe in true love. It's a myth to make the drudgery of child rearing bearable. I'm going to eat my salad before it gets limp and then scout out the ship. You can stay here and feel all philosophical if you want to."

Emma moved reluctantly from the view of the ocean, telling herself she'd get plenty of time to look. "What mindless, meaningless activities are we going to engage in tonight?"

"We're going ashore, girl."

They explored the ship, booked their excursions and

then stopped in the salon to make appointments for manicures and massages. When adventure beckoned, they were going to be ready for it.

2

THAT EVENING Emma could hardly believe she was actually in a bar on the little island of Grand Bahama, lost in the beauty of the local scenery while the sun dipped behind the ocean in a gorgeous sunset that made her glad to be alive.

She felt tingly-nervous. She'd left Tina holed up in a restaurant a few doors down with a handsome man. Tina had been far too preoccupied to be interested in the sunset, or anything else. Emma had felt uncomfortable with the two of them literally falling all over each other.

But wasn't that what she'd come for? To do more than enjoy the sunset? To share it with someone? To find romantic attraction—that spur-of-the-moment, knock-you-off-your-feet sensation?

Fingering the unfamiliar length of her hair, she wondered where to start.

She considered some of Tina's not-so-subtle techniques. If Emma could emulate instead of hesitate then maybe she'd get past all the things that inhibited her.

She'd just pick out a good-looking man and talk to him. But not in the way she'd initiated conversations before.

This time she wanted to pique the guy's interest, the kind of interest that would lead to a night of romantic intimacy.

Only one problem. She tapped her finger against her chin. This meeting couldn't actually lead to an interlude because the passengers were supposed to be back for the captain's cocktail hour at eleven o'clock. The ship sailed again at midnight.

Hmm, a problem, or a practice run?

If she could impress someone here on the island then maybe she could seduce the hell out of a handsome passenger on the ship.

She squared her shoulders. Even Tina would be impressed.

Except she wanted an exotic drink in her hand to set the mood, and to keep the staff off her back while she concentrated on other things. Yes. Some tropical concoction and she'd be ready for anything!

Scanning the bar Emma noted a broad-shouldered, nicely tanned man sitting at a table on the sand. Once she'd worked on that drink, a Latin lover would definitely be the perfect chaser. The man's fit body and wide shoulders were almost too big for the small wicker chair. Dark curling hair waved back in a shaggy, casual style, brushing the collar of the loose, white shirt he wore, and for a minute she fantasized that he looked like a modern-day pirate.

Emma aimed at the empty table well beyond his. Maybe she could just watch him from afar. Consider it the first step.

The second step would be him looking her way, she thought as she headed to the table. She almost stumbled when he did.

And then…

Amazingly, the pirate actually rose to his feet as she approached, grinning in such a friendly fashion it was as if he knew her, and somehow it gave her the courage she needed to pause in front of him.

His gaze was as warm as if he'd physically reached out to her. His smile was incredibly bright on his gorgeous, tanned face. "I saw you enjoying the sunset and I hoped you'd come in closer."

She practically pried her hands from behind her back to offer one to him. "Hi, I'm Emma. You must be from around here. I'm a passenger on a cruise ship, just here for the evening. It's so nice to meet a local. That is, if you are a local—"

She might have babbled on or run away, but he grabbed and squeezed her hand. The tingle she felt stopped her in mid-speech. Is this how initiating a seduction felt? This wonderful, scary feeling, like a roller coaster as you hovered on the arc of the first drop?

"Emma, you spoke so quickly I'm afraid I didn't catch it all."

"Oh, do I have an accent? You don't. It's amazing. I just said that I'm on a cruise and I'm a little…" She started to say nervous but changed her mind. That wasn't the way to pick up a man. This was the perfect opportunity to pretend she was sophisticated, like Tina.

"…thirsty. I'm so thirsty," she said in a rush. "Can you tell me what I should order? I usually order…um… orgasms. You know, the drinks…" Emma almost pinched herself. Had she really been that bold?

FOR TONY, holding Emma's hand was an incredible rush. But hadn't he intended to get Emma out of his system?

"Well," Emma prompted. "What do you locals drink?"

It was the second time she'd suggested he was a local.

Mentally he grinned. A player or a local, either definition would do.

And while he had no idea what language they spoke on the island, he was pretty sure Emma didn't know either. So he'd lean on his Spanish and roll his *R*s, to keep her interested. "I'm…Andres and I know exactly what we should order." He was pleased when his words came out smooth and just slightly accented.

In a throaty purr Emma replied, "Okay, but if you've got a better suggestion then I'd love to, uh, entertain it."

Emma hadn't seemed quite so flirtatious when they'd spoken on the phone. More pragmatic and perhaps a little whimsical. But then she put a hand on his shoulder and distracted him with a single look. No one had prepared him for the kick of those sea-blue eyes.

"I think we can find something appropriately stimulating for a beautiful…mainlander."

"Thank you."

That smile hit him in an interesting place. And when she tried to sit in the minuscule skirt he could have sworn her legs were a million miles long.

The cane material of the chair seemed to grab onto the skirt fabric and he couldn't help but wonder what she wore under the tiny skirt as she fought for balance.

He lifted his hand, wondering how to help, then grabbed on to the back of the chair to keep it from falling over. Emma finally struggled into place, and he settled back, congratulating himself for resisting any peeking while she'd been fixing her skirt.

"What have you been drinking?" Tony asked solicitously. (He had to think of himself as Andres, his middle name, the name his grandmother called him.)

"Nothing, not since lunch."

He was skeptical, but obviously she wasn't driving, so he signaled the waiter and asked for two house specials. The waiter grinned and then went towards the back. The bar was open to the beach, and the salt air, flickering candles and cane furniture gave it an exotic appeal. Andres could feel himself sliding headfirst into the island atmosphere.

"Thank you for ordering the drinks. I'm so excited to be here." Emma grinned at him. "It's like a different world."

He couldn't help himself; he reached out to stroke her hand. The engaging lady from the phone conversations was mesmerizing in person. "It's beautiful."

She blushed. "I do see myself in a whole new light."

"Where's home?"

"Florida."

"And what occupation has you feeling like you needed to visit a new world? Or is it more personal?"

"I'm an administrative assistant for a lawyer, a glorified secretary," she said almost defensively. "But it's not the work or anything else really." She fluttered her hands. "It's my own angst."

He was impressed. "No excuses? No attempt to blame your boss, co-workers, parents, boyfriend or perhaps…husband?"

She touched her ring finger. "No husband, no boy-friend and no one to blame but myself. I just needed a boost."

It had to be that idiot from the office who made her want to get away from it all. "And you've already met one new person," he said with a smile.

"And a very interesting one at that." She licked those incredible lips.

The server slipped the drinks onto the table with an appreciative look toward Emma that she didn't seem to notice.

Andres wondered why she didn't see. Most women collected those kinds of looks like prizes and would have at least preened a bit. But Emma just sat there with those wide eyes focused on him. He wanted to groan when she gave him a provocative smile and re-crossed her legs. One prettily manicured hand slipped casually over to touch his.

Andres took a gulp of the creamy drink to cool off.

He would be privileged to be the only one she had eyes for.

Emma took a long sip from her glass.

Andres avidly watched her mouth. Those full sensuous lips looked so luscious. Then he dropped his gaze to her cocktail wondering if he should tell her there were several shots of hard liquor in that drink, disguised by chocolate and cream. But he only told her what he was thinking, "And you have definitely caught my interest."

She shrugged. "My friend Tina always manages to make life interesting no matter what. And I plan to emulate her."

She swung her foot, gently—nervously?—yet her smile told him that she noticed how his gaze clung to those endless legs. Apparently, she was enjoying his attention.

In person, Emma was intoxicating, like the drink, so sweet you didn't notice it sneaking up and seducing you.

"This will be my voyage of discovery," she said.

Fortunately, another round of drinks arrived to cool him off and he took a large swallow. "What are you hoping to discover?" he asked flippantly, expecting a flirtatious answer.

But she looked pensive for a moment, chewed on her lower lip and then answered very sincerely. "How to be myself and a little more. I just want to crank up the volume. Do you ever feel as if there's something missing from your life and that you might find that something if you were just willing to seize an opportunity?"

Hell yes. Sometimes, at the end of a ten- or twelve-hour session in front of a screen, where he'd only interacted with other human beings via e-mail, he would sit and wonder whether this was the kind of solitary life he wanted. "Yeah, I do."

She sighed. "I'm not sure what I'm missing. But whatever it is, being here with you makes me feel good."

He watched as Emma pulled the large frosty glass toward her and took a healthy swig of the concoction. She took out the umbrella and sucked on the pineapple slice. He ignored his drink, looking at her so intently he wondered if she could feel him wanting to explore her lips first with his avid gaze and then his mouth.

He knew he should be honest and tell her that he wasn't a local.

Would it kill the romantic mood? Or would it be better to play along and see what she had in mind?

She looked up, heat in her gaze.

He definitely wanted to let this ride.

Emma felt as if this handsome local was gazing into her very soul. It was as if they'd already been intimate and he hadn't even touched her or kissed her. And it didn't make any sense. She tried to talk, stumbled, but finally managed, "Um, does this have cocoa in it? I have to admit I'm addicted to chocolate."

"Yes, it's a sort of an island milkshake," he told her.

"It's good. Delectable in fact."

He stroked her hand, his touch gentle yet his skin a little rough, and his warmth sent a shiver through her.

"So how are you going to start this project? Pumping up the volume?" His voice curled around her, seeming to pull her in closer.

She took another deep drink and leaned towards him, then sighed. It felt good to be this close to an incredible guy who obviously found her intriguing.

"You do have a plan," he prompted.

She sat up. She'd been leaning so far over she was practically on top of the table. "Of course I have a plan." A long sip of the milkshake soothed the niggle of embarrassment. *He even understands about the plan. A girl's got to have a plan if she's going to get anywhere.*

"What's the first thing on your list?" It seemed as though he was teasing her now.

"I'm going to explore some aspects of myself that have been…inhibited." She told herself that she was only drunk on his attention.

He looked so intense. Those dark eyes were especially intriguing because a golden band circled his pupils like a little halo of light in the dark.

"That sounds incredibly intriguing."

She reached out to stroke his bare fingers. "I'm not feeling inhibited right now," she told him truthfully.

He reached up to rub a piece of her hair between his fingers, brushing her sensitive ear as he did so.

Her heart paused mid-beat, and she couldn't seem to breathe. Why couldn't he have been a passenger on the cruise?

"What were we talking about?" she muttered.

This pickup thing had been so natural, but what did she do now? She wanted so badly for him to kiss her. How did she signal him? And where would he touch her?

And then what?

This stuff *was* harder than a job interview, even if what she wanted to do had nothing to do with talking.

"We were discussing how a person shouldn't become complacent, that they should, well, rock their world."

"That's a nice thing to say but I'm not very good at that." Emma's brows furrowed as she concentrated. "Just ask my friend Tina. I'm too low-key for that."

"You seem like a woman capable of doing anything she wants, Emma."

To hide the way her lips trembled at his compliment she took another sip of the milkshake. The rum slid down so easily, warming her from the inside, while his words warmed her from the outside. She was getting so hot. Had she ever wanted a man to touch her this badly?

Her nipples were so sensitized that she could feel every brush of the material of her blouse.

"I wish you were on the cruise, too...I mean it's going to be great." She desperately needed him to kiss her. Surely she'd come to her senses once he kissed her.

"I've never wanted anything so much." He stroked her hand and smiled. A smile she just wanted to dive into. *What if I love it when he touches me? What if I don't want him to stop?*

"Are you okay?" he asked solicitously.

Sometimes he sounded so American. Were those alarm bells going off in the distance? "Where are you from?"

"I didn't tell you where I was from, *querida*."

Now that sounded exotic. Did she honestly care where he was from?

She sighed. Touched his hand.

He smiled at her as if she were dear to him, as if she could confide in him. "Why the sigh, *querida*?"

"Lost opportunities." She tilted her head. "Did you ever want to be someone else?" The question hung between them. More honesty. If she didn't quit the sappy stuff, he'd probably walk away. She bit her lower lip nervously.

His gaze clung. "Tonight I want most of all to be able to tell you that I'm a passenger on the cruise."

"Wouldn't that be nice." She sighed again. "Don't even tease me about that."

He looked thoughtful for a moment and then he grinned. "I know, I'll be a pirate, kidnap you and sail away. I'd tie you up in silken bonds and make you very, very happy."

Now that was an image. She leaned towards him again. He did resemble a pirate; she'd thought so from the beginning. "Role-playing never occurred to me." *Except in my fantasies*. "Do you do much role-playing?"

"All the time. I find it enjoyable to add an element of fantasy to life and…love."

Was he blushing? It was hard to tell in the flickering light. She eyed him over her glass. "I'd really like you to kidnap me but I've got to get back to the ship."

"Ah, the cruise ship, an excellent place to find adventure."

"It's the captain's cocktail party tonight," she said, then added before she could take it back, "but I'll be thinking about you."

His eyes gleamed and he put her at ease by saying, "I hope so, because I won't be able to stop thinking about you."

"It's very flattering of you to say so."

"I'm not flattering you. I find you fascinating. You have a cool blond beauty, but I see flickers of fire in those mysterious eyes. I find the contradiction exciting."

Her eyes were mysterious? Probably because they were crossing from too much alcohol. How many shots were in these drinks anyway? Obviously enough to liberate the licentious lady inside. Or was it the way Andres looked at her?

He picked up her hand and held it.

Her stomach flip-flopped and then an ache settled a little lower than her stomach. She rubbed her legs together. She wanted him fiercely.

"What are you thinking?" he asked.

But he knew. His look was equally ravenous.

Emma leaned in. It didn't matter that they were in public. She just wanted a taste—

"Hey, Em?"

Tina approached the table with her long-legged stride and her beautiful confident smile, and Emma's heart sank.

3

"Em, we should get going. We have to get ready for the captain's reception." She held out an elegant hand, "Hi, I'm Emma's friend, Tina."

"I know we have to be back and I've been watching the time." Emma looked at her watch. Then she introduced them. "This is Andres."

Andres gave Tina a very casual look that allowed Emma to breathe again. Tina usually got the attention. Not that she could help it. But tonight it mattered to Emma.

Tina gave Andres a quizzical look.

"Don't I know you?"

"Where would you know me from? Do you come here often?"

"I don't know. You just look familiar. And I'm good at faces."

He grinned. "Maybe I just have one of those faces."

"Maybe."

"What happened to the guy you were with?" Emma asked.

Tina shook her head. "We're going to meet up after the reception. So I won't be in the room tonight. But I thought we would go back to the ship together and get ready. Are you sure you're okay to come alone?"

The old Emma would have hesitated; in fact she probably would have been back at the boat an hour ago, feeling deflated that Tina would be gone their first night on the ship.

But tonight she was definitely different. "I just want to stay a little longer. I won't be late."

"I'll take good care of her." Andres tipped his head at Tina in a very old-style way that must have caught her interest because she hesitated and started to pull out one of the chairs as if she intended to join them.

Abruptly Andres rose to his feet, pulling Emma up with him. "There's a way to go along the beach. I'd like to take Emma that way to show her some of the beauty of our island before she sails away."

"Okay." Did Tina actually look stunned? She just stood there as they left the bar. Emma tried to turn around and say goodbye, but Andres grabbed both of her hands and pulled her along.

"If you give her any encouragement, she'll offer to walk along with us and that's not what I had in mind."

"What do you have in mind?" Alarm bells were going off. She knew she shouldn't go anywhere with a total stranger.

"There's a full moon tonight and I wanted to be with you on the beach."

She just nodded. The thought of walking on the beach sounded too enticing to resist. Like the exotic bar and those drinks. And now the pale sand stretched endlessly before them. Restless, dark water rumbled on the horizon, while lacy froth teased the sand at their feet.

Andres's shoulder felt warm beneath her hands as she

let him steady her while she took off her high-heeled sandals. He offered to carry them for her. His sandals appeared to be waterproof.

Emma's mind filled with exhilarating images of tasting the cocoa concoction on his perfectly shaped lips. She floated along at his side with the warm water sucking gently at her toes.

"It's nice of you to escort me to the docks."

He pulled her around to face him. They'd already left the bar behind. They were totally alone. Shadows lent urgency to his features. "It's not nice at all. It's a matter of need." He ran his fingers through her hair. "I've been dying to touch you. Your hair's like moonlight. And your eyes are like the midnight sky."

His words caressed her. How could such a masculine man say such tender things? "I love the way you talk to me."

"Come on." He pulled her along to the edge of the plunging surf, his eyes more on her than the beautiful view.

"What are you looking at?"

He looked down at her. "You're like some mystical creature from the sea sent to ensnare the poor fisherman. How can I resist you?"

Was that a little grimace of embarrassment on his face? Was it hard for a man to speak in such tender terms? "How romantic you are in the moonlight."

"I'm glad you think so, *chula*."

The foreign word reverberated through her, "And if I were to ensnare you, then what would happen next?"

"I'd follow you wherever you went."

He sounded so sure of himself. It made her nervous and she shivered with anticipation at the same time. "Oh, but you can't follow me onto the ship."

"What if I were to surprise you? Would you be angry or glad? Would you forgive me for wanting to be with you no matter what the cost?"

"I don't know. I think I'd be glad to see you again under any circumstances."

Had he really meant what he'd said about the role-playing fantasy? The image of him taking her as his captive had her tightening her hold on his arm.

"We could explore our fantasies," she said tentatively.

"I would like very much to do so."

Tonight, Emma wondered if she could be bold enough to grab his hands and bring them to her aching breasts. Then she'd step in close enough to press her body against his, to discover if he was also aroused.

When she looked at Andres he was looking at her with a hunger she recognized.

He said something in urgent Spanish.

Though she couldn't understand the words, she understood the tone, and she pushed closer to him, wishing she had the courage to ask for what she wanted, to beg for it. "Please." It came out as a whisper.

He must have heard because he put his head down and rubbed his rough face gently against the side of hers. The need rose inside her, an appetite she'd never had before.

He nibbled on her ear.

She sucked in a breath. Her breasts ached and her nipples tingled.

"Please," she breathed louder.

He bent to touch her lips, giving her a taste of what she hungered for. She felt the sweetness of those soft lips nibbling her skin, and the heat of his tongue tasting her mouth. As the kiss deepened, it fueled her appetite for more of him.

His hands slid down the neckline of her top. His fingers explored the mounds of her breasts, stopping to tease her erect nipples through the thin material.

It was the first time she'd ever gone braless in public and she felt vindicated. Let him dive in and touch her aching flesh. She might never wear a bra again if it felt so good to invite a stranger's touch.

He kissed her again, dragging her down with him in a relentless undertow of heady pleasure. When she surfaced his hands were under her top caressing her breasts. She panted. It was happening so fast and so fiercely. She needed him to touch her everywhere.

"Will you take off your top for me? I want to see your breasts in the moonlight."

"Someone will see." The idea seemed so outrageous and yet she longed to be naked, caressed by his hand and the moonlight.

"There's no one around, *chulita*."

The exotic word sent shivers through her, though she could only guess what it meant.

He urged her top up and Emma pulled one arm out of her sleeve and then the other. She dropped it carelessly onto the sand as Andres lowered his face to her breasts. He used both hands to caress her nipples and then he took one of them into his mouth and suckled her.

She curled her toes in the sand, while clinging to his shoulders, his shirt buttons hard against her naked stomach. When he laved the other nipple the breeze teased her and she shuddered.

Sensation lapped her in waves. She held on tighter.

"You taste so good, *chula*. Do you taste this good everywhere?"

She didn't know how to answer him. How far did they dare to go? What did he want? As if in answer to her question he ran his hands down her naked abdomen, briefly teasing the sensitive skin at her navel, and then slid them around her hips, to cup her bottom. Pressed against his erection, Emma nestled closer. The little short skirt was hiked up between them and his hand stroked her cheeks, exposed by her thong.

"Ah, this is nice. I like the thong. I'd like to move it aside and tease the sweet flesh beneath it."

Emma gasped the word this time. "Please."

Andres took her mouth even more deeply and she melted against him. She would give him everything if he just slid his fingers closer to where she needed them to be.

Please just touch me there.

Those clever fingers must have read her mind because he ran them over the silk of her thong.

Once. Then again. Until the material was thoroughly saturated.

"You like this, *chulita*. I can feel you shudder sweetly beneath my hand."

Unable even to nod, knees barely supporting her, arms wrapped around his shoulders, Emma held on for dear life. And when his fingers finally pushed the thong aside and teased her clitoris, she almost sobbed.

He stroked her, murmuring Spanish words in her ear, holding her securely as she approached the edge.

And then pulling back.

The thong slid into place, now a very sensitive place, and her hips twitched. She would have protested but he teased her nipple with clever fingers, pulling gently, then kneading.

She tried to gasp and catch her breath at the same time. Could she protest that he hadn't satisfied her? She certainly wanted him to.

"You're so sweet, *chulita.* So seductive. Like the cream on those sweet drinks you like so well." He lowered his head to take her nipple into his mouth, and at the same time he slid his hand back down to nestle on top of the thong.

Emma couldn't resist. She ran her hand over the front of his shorts. His erection was huge and she pushed against it, rubbing him, wishing there were somewhere that they could have sex, the kind of sex where he was deep inside her.

He groaned, then pushed the thong all the way down until it caught on the bend of one of her knees.

Emma's breath swooshed out of her as she realized they needed a condom. How could she have left the room without one? She just hadn't thought… "I don't have any protection with me," she whispered, wanting to cry at the thought of him dumping her on the sand to find a woman that would satisfy him.

That huge erection, those exotic love words…all she

wanted was to lie down in the sand and have him for herself. But the risks lined up like bullets in her head.

"Shh, *chula*. I'll take care of you."

She held her breath, afraid, intrigued and hoping he meant that he had a condom and not that she would have to fend him off.

His fingers brushed against the surface of her clit, teasing.

Emma forgot the condom problem. She arched against his fingers, whimpering, begging with her body language for something she'd never be able to ask for with words.

He pushed his fingers inside of her, deeper. She pushed back, wanting him. She rubbed his cock beneath his shorts with short hard strokes, imagining it inside her.

He stroked her in an uneven, thrusting rhythm that was somehow just right. Deep, hard and yet she felt secure enough in his grasp to let go to the point where she couldn't think, could only push back with her hips against that incredible pressure!

He said something more in what she assumed was Spanish. She begged, almost sobbing with need and on the verge of something miraculous.

"Come for me, *amorsito*."

She crested with a little scream.

Emma could barely lift her head. Her thong had fallen to the sand, her body throbbed, and her breasts burned, with the breeze still teasing them.

He held her close, petting her butt cheeks, pulling her skirt down, caressing her quivering belly.

Breathing hard, she tried to orient herself. She was

on a beach with a stranger who'd just given her a mind-blowing orgasm. Surprisingly, Emma didn't want to waste time examining anything. What she did wonder was if it had to be over or could they...

Her watch beeped.

"I think you should try to stand by yourself or else you'll miss the cocktail party." His voice sounded gravelly.

She could feel him trembling. It made her bold as she'd never been before. "No, I set the alarm twenty minutes ahead."

He laughed hoarsely. "Passionate and organized. You're an incredible woman. I'll get you to the ship. I know you're looking forward to the party." He pulled away from her slowly as if afraid she might topple over.

Her legs held her, barely. She almost lost it when he bent down and picked up her thong out of the sand between her legs. She stepped out of it, he looked at her, and then he put the thong in his pants pocket.

Emma opened her mouth to protest. The little bulge of her thong rested next to another, larger bulge. What could she say? How arousing it was that he wanted to keep the thong, even if it meant going back to the ship with the breeze tantalizing her already sensitized flesh under that tiny skirt? Had she honestly let this stranger touch her intimately with his fingers?

Not only had she allowed that to happen, she intended it to happen again. She began untangling the problem.

"Can you hand me my shirt, *please?*" The *please* reminded her of her outrageous behavior and she smiled happily. She'd done it. She'd had a fling. And what an amazing fling.

Andres held up her shirt. As she leaned forward to take it from him, his hand skimmed over her nipples.

"I don't know. I like you bare. You're truly beautiful illuminated by moonlight."

Emma barely managed not to drag him down on the sand and have her way with him.

"I want you to come back to the ship with me." It came out in a rush. "Please."

"But locals are not allowed on board."

"The hell with it. We'll think of something."

"And your fancy reception?"

"My roommate won't miss me and she's not coming back to the room tonight." One problem solved. One more to go.

"Are you sure?"

"Hmm, let me think. Do I want to have you alone in my room or go to a reception? For once I'm going to do exactly what I want. And I want you to make me feel like you just did, and more. We'll only be on your island for a few more hours and I want you with me, all the way with me." She reached out and brushed the front of his shorts.

He was definitely taken with the idea. If anything he was harder than before.

Still, for a moment she held her breath, frightened he would refuse her outrageous offer. But his smile said it all. He took her hand and they hurried silently along the beach, rapidly approaching the lights of the harbor.

Emma caught her breath and tried to regain her composure. *I should feel ashamed of myself.* But all she could feel was the throbbing between her legs and her heart stammering. A sexy, outrageous woman had been born on that beach and she wasn't ready to let go of that, at least for a few hours—unless, of course, they put her in the brig for trying to smuggle Andres on board.

As they arrived at the harbor Emma caught her breath at the sight of the huge ship, strung with lights like a giant Christmas tree. "It still feels a bit unreal to be on a cruise," she murmured. "Like being in a movie or something."

"As long as it's not *Titanic*," he teased.

She laughed. "I think we're safe. I don't see Leonardo DiCaprio anywhere," she said pretending to look around.

"No Kate Winslet either," he said, then turned those dark eyes her way. They gleamed at her with obvious appreciation and he stroked her face. "Just you."

She shivered. "Now we have to get you aboard."

"Just how do you intend to get me aboard?"

"Distraction. I'm thinking I'm going to have to distract the guy looking at the identification. I'll scratch my leg and lift my skirt or something." She tried to imagine what Tina would do in her situation.

Andres looked pensive. "Do you know who your chef is? The main one? They advertise it. Is it the British guy, Jonathan Sparks?"

"I think so. It sounds familiar. How do you know?"

"He, uh, comes into the bar where you met me, occasionally. He's cool. He might help me or it might be okay if I go up to the staff entrance. I'll just say I'm going to visit him. Guys I know do it all the time to get on board to visit women."

"And you don't?"

"I hadn't found you."

She leaned against his arm, wanting to be convinced. "If you can get on the ship I'll be so grateful. But it doesn't make any sense…"

He very discreetly ran the fingers of one hand over her nipples where her breasts were pressed against his other arm. "I'll be very convincing. I really want to be with you, *querida*."

"Okay." She sighed, unable to breathe, let alone think, with him playing with her body, and again so glad she hadn't worn a bra. "I'm in cabin F55." She leaned closer to give him better access. Luckily there were only a few people around them. Probably most had gone to the captain's reception already, or they were still exploring in town.

He tugged on one beaded nipple through her shirt. "I'm going to suckle you until you scream. I want to see how a drink tastes when I lap it off of your skin. When you get to your room, order one of those milkshakes from room service and I'll show you what cocoa and cream are for."

Nodding dumbly, she could feel her eyes almost crossing with desire while her normally practical brain seemed to have gone on permanent vacation.

Andres leaned down and kissed her cheek. "*Chula,* you wait here for fifteen minutes. If I don't come back, you'll know I made it onto the ship."

She nodded.

He grinned and then gave her breasts one last pat before untangling himself from her side.

Emma felt as though she was floating while she waited to see if he'd come back. Everything seemed distant and just a little unreal. The thought of him meeting her at her room had her almost dizzy with delight. This was the adventure of a lifetime.

Her watch timer interrupted her musings and she looked around one last time to make sure Andres wasn't coming before she boarded the ship. The man who took her ship's identification gave her a warm smile. "Miss, the captain's reception has just begun if you'd like to attend." He handed her back her identification.

"Thank you. But I'm a little tired. I think I'll just go back to my room."

"As you wish." He was cute, probably Italian. There seemed to be a lot of Italian men among the crew.

"Thank you." Emma smiled to herself.

He grinned back flirtatiously.

Her feet barely touched the ground as she headed to her cabin.

Emma avoided the beautiful, sculpted center staircase with its lighted banister winding like a Christmas ribbon up and down the ship levels. It would be packed with people in sparkling gowns and tuxedos on their way to and from the reception. Normally she wouldn't have missed such an exciting experience, but she had a very hot date. She took the elevator without a shred of remorse.

Usually, Emma handled anything mechanical with

ease, but tonight her hands trembled, so she had trouble sliding the key card for her room into the door slot. Her flesh tingled and her heart fluttered.

She got into the room and then paused as the door sealed shut behind her. What to do now? She remembered Andres's promise to sip the drink off her flesh, and her nipples hardened into knots. Emma grabbed the room-service menu off the desk. She ran her finger down the drink selections and found a Mocha Meltdown, the description almost fitting the drink she'd just had in the bar on the beach.

She picked up the phone and ordered two of them in a voice that quavered; they probably thought she was already tipsy, but what the hell. She put the phone down and sank onto her bunk. How would the cold concoction feel on her flesh, and where exactly did Andres plan to put it?

She shivered.

Then she jumped up and headed for the bathroom. She didn't have time for a shower but she could sponge down a bit. Leaving the door cracked open, she took a washcloth and ran it under warm water. Then she pulled her shirt over her head. Her breasts felt so full and perky. They seemed to swell when she ran the cloth over them. She sucked in her breath as her sensitive flesh responded, her knotted nipples aching.

After unfastening her skirt and pulling it down to let it fall to the ground, she put the washcloth between her legs to cool the heated flesh. Her knees felt unsteady as she thought of him thrusting into her.

After the milkshake.

Did she dare suggest such a thing or would she even have to?

Naked and freshened she went to Tina's suitcase and borrowed a flirty little silk robe in a hibiscus print. Back in the bathroom she put on some eye shadow and mascara. He wouldn't be able to stay long because the boat sailed right after the reception, sometime around midnight. Emma figured she wouldn't have time to get raccoon eyes. She shook out her hair and brushed it, enjoying the way her newly straightened locks swung around her head.

I look pretty, she thought. *I have that glow. Anyone seeing me would know what I've been up to. And I want more of it.* She smiled at the wanton in the mirror.

And she was going to enjoy every minute of it.

She put the hairbrush down, beginning to worry that Andres hadn't made it on board after all when she remembered the condoms. *Better put them under the pillow. Wouldn't want to have to stop in the middle of things.* She giggled, feeling like a crazy woman.

Tina had brought a huge variety of condoms. She'd even bought some that glowed in the dark. Emma held one of the packages thinking it was a shame that she didn't have the guts to suggest a glow-in-the-dark condom. Instead she took out three of the gold ones, ribbed, and put them under her pillow.

Then she went back and got two more.

A knock on the door startled her and she jumped up and ran to answer it.

Andres stood in the hallway looking incredibly proud of himself. His grin went straight to her guts.

"You did it!" She pulled him into the room by his arm. "I was getting worried. Especially since it dawned on me that the chef would surely be showing off his expertise tonight for the captain's reception. How did you get in?"

"I saw another guy I know from the ship. These guys come onto the island all the time. Anyway, uh, Santos, he let me come aboard."

Emma didn't know what to do with herself so she sort of leaned against the edge of the desk, which was bolted to the wall. "Oh, I guess they must get shore leave or something. I just thought they worked during the cruise."

"The ships come to the island for supplies between cruises. Maybe that's when they come by the bar." He took the few steps separating them in the cabin, which suddenly seemed small and intimate. "Do you want to discuss the shore leave of the ship's staff right now, when we only have a couple of hours?"

She shook her head.

He put his finger on her thigh and ran it up under the edge of the silk robe. "This is gorgeous on you."

She shivered at his touch. "Thank you."

His finger climbed higher on her thigh.

Emma scooted back onto the desk.

He pressed closer until his hand cupped her between the legs. He rubbed her gently, back and forth.

Immediately Emma could feel her brain turn to mush. Andres was right. It didn't matter how he'd gotten on the ship. She wanted, needed him to finish what he'd started on the beach.

"You're so responsive. I love the way those baby

blues go all hazy when I touch you here. I can tell when that brain stops clicking and you go all soft and womanly on me. Your intelligence is a turn-on, but I love it when you let me turn on this part of you." He found the perfect spot with one of those clever fingers and pressed deeply.

"Oh." She parted her lips to let the soft sound emerge and he leaned down to kiss her. His lips were perfectly shaped and soft. He tasted her and then pulled away to nibble her bottom lip.

"Do you like this, sweetheart?"

She wanted him to call her *chula* or *chulita* or any of the Spanish love words that made him so exotic but all she could do was kiss him avidly. The pressure on her clitoris had all her attention. The sweet insanity of his touch made her long for more.

Reaching out, she ran her hand down the front of his shorts.

He rocked his finger back and forth. Emma rocked back and forth.

Her lips parted inviting his tongue, and he thrust into her mouth. At the same moment she cried out. As she came in his arms, he held her closely.

When she gathered all the brain cells he'd scattered with his lovemaking, she realized she had just come perched on the edge of a desk. Emma tried desperately to think if she'd ever been this easy to seduce.

"You are so orgasmic. I love to watch you, sweetheart."

Orgasmic? Was he kidding? "I guess you know how to touch me. It must be your Latin blood."

"Well, yes…*chula*. It's probably my Latin blood."

She gestured weakly towards the bed. "That bunk is

mine," she said a bit awkwardly. "I've got some condoms under my pillow."

Andres immediately put her at ease. "Let's just focus on your pleasure right now," he told her. "I want those eyes fuzzy with desire." He bent down and took her nipple into his mouth through the thin silk robe. In a moment there was a wet spot over her aching breast. He moved back and blew gently on the spot.

Emma shivered. "That feels so wonderful."

He suckled her again and with the other hand he plucked her distended nipple.

She arched her back. He was just firm enough, his mouth and fingers sending ripples through her. Her heart rate soared. She wanted him to take her to the bunk. "Andres."

Then there was a knock on the door.

Andres smiled at her. "Did you order drinks for us, *querida?*"

She just nodded. She didn't know how much more stimulation she could handle. She just wanted him to ravish her with his cock. Now!

"I'll answer the door. I don't want anyone else to see you. You're so beautiful and I want it to be just for me."

He sounded so possessive.

It's just lover talk, not a proposal.

"Okay. I'll just slip behind here."

He went to the door. Emma pulled the robe closer and stepped behind the bathroom door. She tried to figure out a good place to suggest they have the drinks. Would he really lay her down and use the milkshake on her? She shivered at the thought. Sweets during sex. Only a bold, sexy woman would do something like that—the woman she intended to become, here in his arms.

He shut the door and then walked past her to put the drinks down on the little nightstand by her bunk. "Come to me, *chulita*."

On weak knees she wobbled the few steps to his arms. He enfolded her. "I wish you were a passenger on the ship," she whispered in his ear.

He leaned down and kissed her gently. "So do I, sweetheart."

"I like it better when you call me *chulita*. It reminds me that I'm with a sexy foreign man."

He reached down and took something out of one of the drinks. He offered it to her. It was a piece of pineapple dipped in chocolate. "Here, *chula*."

She took a little bite and he kissed her, sliding his tongue into her mouth to taste the treat, at the same time running his hands down her body over the silky robe.

"Um, you taste so good."

"Mmm." She had to agree. They tasted so good together. She tugged on the hem of his shirt and then ran her fingers up over his belly and to his wide chest. "I want to feel you. Please take this off."

He gave her one last kiss and then stripped off his shirt. His tanned, muscled chest looked incredibly good. He had almost no chest hair, just a little trail below his belly button that disappeared into his waistband. She rubbed his erection through his shorts. He was so hard.

"The shorts, now, take off your shorts."

"Shh, the milkshake will melt."

"What are you going to do with it?"

He went past her into the bathroom and came out with a fluffy white towel. "You better put this under you, *amorsito.*"

She could feel her eyes widen. This might get embarrassing. What the heck was she doing with a total stranger in a stateroom with a milkshake?

But she didn't want to stop. Besides the apprehension in her middle, there was an insistent ache elsewhere that made her want to draw closer.

His grin told her that he'd caught her uncertainty.

"We'll do the hard-core fantasy stuff some other time, after I've tied you up and carried you off the ship and made you a prisoner on my island."

"That sounds good," Emma choked out.

"Come here, *chula.*" He beckoned. "This is going to feel good, I promise."

Still, she hesitated when everything in her urged her to rush to his arms.

"All I want to do is taste this drink on your perfect skin. Please, Emma. Trust me." He reached for the tie on her robe. "May I take off your robe?"

How sweetly he asked her. She obediently put her hands up to the tie on her robe, but he stopped her before she could untie it.

Slowly, looking down into her eyes, he untied the robe, letting the silk flutter to the floor.

"You're so beautiful." His voice sounded thick.

She certainly felt beautiful to have such a huge effect on him.

He slid his arms around her shoulders and then scooped up her legs at the knees. She snuggled against his chest. As Andres laid her gently on her bunk, he stared down at her as if she were the only person in his world. She reached up to run her hand down the trail of dark hair and over his erection.

He sucked in his breath.

"I do trust you and I really, really want you to come here and be with me." Yet she couldn't help but curl up her body, hiding it from his stare. She felt so naked.

"You trust me? Honestly?"

She nodded.

"Then open to me. Lie on your back, please, *amorsito*."

Hesitantly, she moved so that she lay on her back. Legs stretched out, breasts and belly vulnerable. Nervous, thrilled, wet and waiting.

He took a sip of the drink and leaned down, his gaze never leaving her face. Then he kissed her, the taste of the cocoa liquor exploding in her mouth. His fingers explored her from her breasts to her pubis, and when she was gasping for breath, those fingers cupped her moist, aching flesh.

Her legs fell open.

Frustration and need had her arching up to meet his next kiss, drinking deeply from him.

"Oh Andres."

As he petted her, she reached out to stroke his cock, trying to give him the same intense pleasure his touch aroused in her.

"Oh, I'm so ready for you." Forget the milkshake. She'd never been more ready to have a man thrusting inside her. The ache was so profound it almost hurt.

He moved her hand. "I can't think when you touch me, *chula*."

"Neither can I," she breathed.

"Good. Because I just want you to feel this. I want to take you to heaven with me."

She opened her eyes in time to see him pour a little of the liquor on her belly where it pooled in her navel. She shuddered when the coolness touched her heated skin, but remained still, so it wouldn't spill. Then he took the spoon off of the tray. His eyes met hers with dark intensity, the same beautiful brown as the drink. With the spoon, he scooped out some of the drink from the glass and put it on his tongue.

Then he reached down to kiss her.

She met him halfway, hungry for him and unconcerned as the liquor rolled over the skin of her belly, down around her waist. His tongue rolled over hers, sweet, strong and so heady.

He pulled back. "Now you've made a mess." He reached down and laved the liquor from her skin in slow strokes.

Emma watched him avidly.

Those dark eyes were full of desire and patience. It was so sexy.

He wasn't touching her anywhere but the skin of her abdomen, but she couldn't breathe, wanting to scream with the power of wanting him. Had it ever been this intense?

"Ah, that feels so incredible."

"I can't tell you how good you taste, *amorsito*."

"I want you. Please."

"Please give me a few minutes. I want to enjoy the way you respond to me. I've been dreaming about you."

"Dreaming?" she murmured.

He cleared his throat. "Uh, dreaming of a lover who responds to my every touch."

He left her and she almost sobbed with frustration. "Come back. I need to feel you."

"There's just enough left in this glass."

Her eyes flew open. He stood over her with the spoon and milkshake. "I want you to bend your legs and tilt your hips up, please, *chula.*"

"Are you sure…?" She felt so vulnerable and yet she trusted him.

"Please."

She did as he asked and the cool spoon touched her gently, just inside of her vagina. Then the cool sensation became cold, and the chill bit into her flesh. She sucked in her breath. "Andres, it's too cold."

Shaking with reaction, she curled her arms around herself. "It's too much," she protested and it was, but there was a curious pleasure with the pang.

Her hips twitched. She shuddered. Suddenly, just when it became too much, he licked the cream off her clitoris with hot strokes of his tongue.

His mouth felt so fiery after the freezing cold of the drink.

Emma sucked in a breath, feeling as though she would suffocate, but who needed to breathe? She sobbed instead, arching her body as he gave her all of his attention, licking and suckling.

Her flesh was quickly warm again and so sensitized

by the combination of cold and hot, she quivered, shivered and shuddered, heading for the edge. But he pulled away.

Emma moaned in protest.

"Shhh, *chulita*. I'm not finished with my dessert."

He put another spoonful of the burning cold, milk-shake just inside her vagina, and Emma thought she might scream this time as the warmth she'd gained frosted over. Pleasure as sharp as ice shot through her, and only the heat of his mouth on her clitoris saved her.

But this time he didn't stop laving her. And while he suckled her clit, he gently pushed the handle end of the spoon inside her body, sending her over the edge into a sweet, frothy oblivion.

Emma surfaced, slowly, to see Andres putting a condom on his cock.

She ran her fingers down the ribbed latex. "I want to feel you inside of me. You can be *my* dessert," she finished, thrilled that she could actually tell him such an intimate thing.

He stood over her and ran his hands in little circles around her nipples.

"I've wanted you from the minute I saw you in that bar." She arched as his touch centered on her nipples. "Ah, you are so good with your hands…and the spoon."

"Hmm, it's you, *chula*. I don't think I've ever made love to such a responsive woman." He bent down to kiss her deeply. "Tonight, you've given me so much."

What Andres said washed over her in a warm wave. But she had to remind herself this was only a fling, and he probably said that to all of the women he made love to.

He put one leg over hers and joined her on the bed. Emma arched up to feel his skin pressed against her but he only pulled away. "Just a minute, *chula*. I need to feel you."

He ran his hand between her legs. "You feel so incredible. Are you ready?"

She grabbed hold of his cock and squeezed hard, rubbing back and forth over the latex.

He groaned. "If you keep that up I won't be able to resist you."

"Don't resist! Please," she gasped, holding the tip of him tightly, trying to make him want her as desperately as she desired him. And she yearned for something, something she sensed only he could give to her.

He pushed her hands aside and straddled her hips. Then he pushed his engorged cock into her body slowly, then more firmly as her flesh parted for him.

Though she thought he would be spent in a few minutes he once again proved himself a masterful lover, thrusting until he had her at the edge of the world and then slowing down until she begged and writhed beneath him.

Finally, he pinned her to the bunk with forcible thrusts, filling the hungry void in her body with an orgasm so intense it pulled a true scream from her.

4

THE SHIP BELLS woke Emma from her brief nap and she rolled over with the towel draped over her hips. The chocolate stain on the towel reminded her that the interlude with Andres hadn't been a dream. She stretched luxuriously. She hadn't felt this good in years. Every inch of her felt good. Sated and satisfied. Better than a massage, better than anything.

But now the dark cabin seemed so empty.

And though she felt content, there was a little ache in her heart. Emma rubbed the center of her chest. There could be no heart involved in this experiment. She couldn't afford to get stomped on again.

This was about breaking out of her traditional, self-imposed, heavily regulated and overly cautious life. This was about exploring the spontaneous side of her nature, including the sensual woman she'd been last night. This was not about getting attached.

And she'd done so well with everything else, she had no intention of making that mistake—not that she'd get the chance.

She lifted her head and looked around. Had he left her a note or anything? Maybe his name and address.

They could e-mail and she could fly to see him. She hurried over to the desk, holding the towel around her waist. On the mirror he'd drawn a heart with a tube of Tina's bright-red lipstick. It was romantic and sweet but she'd been hoping for something more practical. She silently berated herself for already letting her resolve slip.

"Take a shower and put this in perspective," she said, looking at herself through the lipstick heart. "Tina will be back soon."

Emma looked around for evidence of their lovemaking but Andres had apparently cleaned up everything except one of the drink cups half full of melted milkshake. Emma swallowed the rest of the drink. Then she opened the door to the balcony to let the night air sweep the smell of sex from the room. There was a lot of commotion outside and she assumed they were preparing to get under way.

It's after midnight and tonight I feel like a princess instead of like the pumpkin, thanks to Andres.

She wrapped her arms around her waist. She'd done it, broken through inhibitions and expanded her horizons. The dark water shimmered with reflecting light. It really was a voyage of discovery.

With one last look at the harbor for a tall, dark and handsome man, she bowed her head and then went to take a hot shower.

Feeling exhausted and let down once she got out of the shower, Emma sat down on her bunk with a sigh. A minute later Tina blew in like a whirlwind.

"Well girl, you certainly did well on your first night

out. That Latino was hot. Amazing. I couldn't have done better myself. Did he whisper naughty Spanish words in your ear? Did he have his way with you back in the men's room at the bar?"

"You've actually had sex in a men's room?"

"Never, I prefer the ladies' room. It's cleaner."

Emma giggled. Tonight she wished she'd thought of such an outrageous thing.

Tina put her purse down on her bunk. "I like that little smirk. What gives?"

"You look gorgeous. How was the captain's reception?"

"Okay, so you're not quite ready to give up the dirt."

"You first."

Tina shrugged her wrap off her bare shoulders. "Okay, the captain's too old to be interesting but I've got my eye on this handsome Italian safety officer. He's got the cutest accent and a gleam in his eye. I'm not sure if they have a fraternizations rule or not, but if they do I'll bet he's willing to break it." She twirled around and the sequins on her halter top caught the light. Then she kicked off her red do-me pumps. "Oh and I saw a lawyer I know."

"So what are you doing back here if you've got a lawyer and the safety officer panting after you?" Emma asked her. "I thought you were going to spend the night with the guy from the bar."

"The lawyer's not after me. He's a colleague and absolutely off-limits. Besides I was worried about you. I wondered if you'd missed the boat messing around in the men's room. You did say you were going to the captain's reception."

"I got a better offer." Andres might be gone but she had something priceless from him—the memory of seizing the moment and finding it more than she'd ever imagined it could be. Maybe that's why the sex had been so great.

"I don't believe I've ever seen that particular smile on your face before. Do you have him stashed under the bunk?"

"It was better than the ladies' room, that's for sure."

"What?"

"We made out on the beach on the way to the ship. It was, well, incredible."

"No way!" Tina rushed over to sit on the bunk beside Emma.

Emma nodded. "Yep."

"And…?"

"It was so good that I smuggled him on board and had my wild way with him."

"Here? Tonight?"

"You wouldn't believe it if I told you about it." Emma crossed her hands over her chest. "I'm still giddy."

"Was it that good?"

"He was amazing. I didn't realize you could do such erotic things with a milkshake."

Tina's eyes widened and she laughed aloud. "Milkshake? Where did you get the milkshake? And the gumption? I'm so proud of you, girl."

"Mocha Meltdowns—they're wonderful drinks that go down so smooth you never feel the jolt." She felt herself blush, but this stuff was too good not to share.

"Too bad you had to leave him behind." She looked

around. "You *did* leave him behind. He's not hiding out on the balcony or anything, is he?"

Emma shook her head reluctantly.

"How on earth did you get him here? With all of the security, I'm shocked he made it aboard."

"Well, I thought I might have to pretend I was you and lift my skirt to distract the porter checking our identification. It might have worked, especially since Andres had my thong in his pocket. But Andres knew some of the staff on the ship and he was able to get in through the staff entrance."

Tina looked a bit pensive. "I guess it's possible he knows someone on the staff."

"He mentioned the chef."

Tina rubbed her hand over her stomach. "The chef *is* amazing. I'm sorry you missed his lobster canapés. But I'm sure the *dessert* you had more than made up for the loss of a little lobster."

Emma reached over and hugged her friend. "Thank you so much for bringing me on this cruise, Tina. I can never repay you for what you've done for me tonight."

"Sounds like Andres did all of the work."

"But you encouraged me to try new things and stop examining everything to death. So instead of being overly cautious, I just let myself go with Andres. Nothing crossed my mind—I was completely swept up from the first time I saw him."

"I could tell."

"Tonight I didn't think. I wanted him so badly and I didn't have a condom and so I just went for it. I couldn't have done it without your encouragement."

"You didn't, not without a condom!" Tina grabbed Emma's hands.

Emma laughed and covered her hands affectionately. "I'm not stupid. That's why I dragged him on board, so I could have my way with him safely, with your large supply of condoms. It was wonderful."

"Okay, okay. So I admit I'm envious. You make my Italian safety officer seem awfully tame in comparison." Tina got up off the bunk and smoothed the back of her dress. "Well, now you should come to the club and find someone to put out that fire for you. We both could use a little dancing and debauchery."

Emma took a deep breath. "No, not tonight. I think I'll stay in. I've had enough excitement to last me a while." A little shiver passed through her. "I even told him that truth."

"What truth?"

"You know. You mentioned that I should tell something I'd never admitted before and so I did."

"What?"

"Essentially I told him that I wanted to pump up the volume, just be more of myself." She leaned forward and tapped her finger on her chin. "And you know what, Tina?"

"What?"

"In that moment I realized that I actually like myself. I don't want to change. I just want to get rid of a few inhibitions and incorporate some new ways to express myself." She sat back. "Is that weird?"

Tina smiled. "No, it's great. More people should admit that they like themselves. It's the key to confidence. Then there wouldn't be so many miserable people raining their misery down on everyone around them."

Emma knew this was a bit from Tina's childhood. While Emma's home life had been wonderful as a beloved only child, Tina had not been so lucky. Only when Emma's world had fallen apart after her parents' divorce a few years ago had Emma begun to understand a little of Tina's perspective.

Tina spotted her lipstick on the mirror. "The heart's a nice touch. I guess he likes you, too." Her eyes met Emma's in the reflection. "Maybe he's an entrepreneur who's made a lot of money and retired to the islands. Too bad he didn't leave you an e-mail address instead of a heart." She winked.

"I thought the same thing." Emma sounded pitiful even to herself. "I would have saved up and visited him— whether he's a entrepreneur or just a poor beach bum."

Tina picked up the tube, rolled up the lipstick and wiped it with a tissue, and then applied the fire-engine red with a pretty purse of her lips. When she was done she looked at Emma in the mirror. "You said you were going to get some action, and you did. So come on. Are you sure you don't want to go out? You don't want to sleep alone tonight."

"Yes, I want to sleep alone tonight. I want to be able to dream about him." Emma wrapped her hands around herself.

"You certainly have it bad. Or maybe you just had it too good." Tina looked down at the brochures on the desk. She picked one up and Emma could see it was the one with the picture of the hot tub on the front. She looked thoughtful. "And how many of those condoms did you use? Do we still have some of the glow-in-the-dark ones?"

"Yeah, we've got the glow-in-the-dark and a bunch of others still. Jeez, you must have brought forty condoms."

"A girl can never be too prepared. I'm thinking the glowing condoms might be interesting in the hot tub in the middle of the night but I think the safety officer said they drain the hot tubs around eleven o'clock. What a disappointment."

"Yeah, that's a bummer," Emma echoed, preoccupied with the image of Andres in a hot tub dressed only in a glowing condom. "Wow."

"Close your mouth, honey. You're drooling."

Emma snapped her mouth shut. "I guess both the hot tub and the gorgeous exotic man are both out of reach, at least on this cruise."

"There are other men on board. I saw quite a few during the captain's reception. And they looked great. As yummy as the hors d'oeuvres."

"I promise I'll start scoping out the other men first thing tomorrow."

"Okay, but I'm only letting you off the hook because you already hit the jackpot tonight." Tina left in the same whirlwind style in which she'd arrived.

Emma, feeling restless, wandered around the room. Then she settled down on a corner of Tina's bed to fold all of the clothes Tina had left draped over her bed.

The dusk till dawn movie proved to be a romantic comedy that didn't hold her interest, so after she changed into her bedtime tank and shorts, Emma sat on the balcony with her feet against the rail. The sea was illuminated by the moon and she watched the dark waves. Resigned to a lonely night, she closed the curtain and tucked herself into her bunk.

EMMA LAY in the sun on a lounge chair, physically resisting the urge to pull at the thong and uncomfortably aware of the sun warming the virgin flesh of her bottom. *I can't believe I'm dressed like this, or rather, undressed.*

Although it felt kinda airy.

Just then a good-looking man passed by, looking down at her with a smile.

She smiled back, gamely. *I hope he didn't notice that little bit of cellulite under my butt cheeks.*

Another man passed and Emma's smile was starting to feel like a grimace. *This is exhausting.*

She picked up her head and looked around. No one seemed to be zeroing in on her. Good, she could tell Tina she'd smiled at all the men who looked her way even though it felt more like work than fun. Wasn't this attraction stuff supposed to be instant and magical?

Like last night?

She closed her eyes and let her breathing deepen. She'd actually downed a couple of Tylenol PM with her lunch, hoping for a little nap. Tina would surely drag her out tonight and she hadn't been able to sleep last night for thinking of Andres.

Eventually, the music and noise of the ship faded away, like the white noise of the ship's engine. It felt as if she was lying right on the water, being rocked like a child. Slowly she descended through the water. Little fish darted around her and nibbled on her toes until she finally tumbled into the dark.

For a moment she felt lost.

Then Andres called her name. He pulled her from the depths with a few flips of his sinewy merman's tail. Without a pause they were basking in the sunlight and he was entirely human, naked and aroused.

"Here, let me help you adjust the chair." He bent and raised the back of the lounge just enough that she'd be comfortable, lightly touching her shoulders and brushing against her front as he did so. The umbrella above her head was bright red and the beach just a few feet away was misty with sea spray.

"What are we doing here?" She asked. "I fell into the depths."

"Isn't the ocean beautiful today? It's exactly the color of your eyes."

"Thanks." She felt breathless. "Are we on another island?"

"Do you want some help with that bikini?" He looked at her top. "Isn't this a topless beach?"

She looked around and saw two women sunning their breasts on beach towels in the sand.

She felt herself blush, but he'd already seen her breasts and she really wanted to feel the sun on her skin. She reached behind her and unhooked the bikini top. It fell to her waist.

He looked avidly at her breasts. Then he reached for the sunscreen. "You don't want to sunburn those nipples. It might hurt."

Emma looked around for the topless women, but

they'd disappeared, and she and Andres had the beach to themselves. She nodded, indicating he could use the sunscreen on her. Her nipples stood up as if they were begging for more than sunscreen.

He sat down on the edge of the lounge, leaning forward to put his hands on her breasts. Then he began to caress around the nipples, carefully massaging her needy flesh. "Andres," she protested.

"I don't think this coconut sunscreen could possibly taste as good as you do." He bent down to lick her aroused flesh. She shuddered.

Leaning over her, he tugged her thong up, putting sweet pressure on her clit. She moaned and tried to get closer to him. But he kept moving away. Further and further away.

"Emma, you're going to burn if you don't put on more sunscreen."

Tina watched with amusement as Emma's eyes shot open and she blinked, obviously trying to orient herself. They were lying on lounge chairs in the middle of the ship's main deck, surrounded by people, good music and lots of handsome waiters in uniform. And apparently Emma had been bored enough to sleep. "Emma? Were you asleep?"

Emma just nodded. She lifted her head and looked confusedly at the pool.

"Emma?"

"I'm just a little groggy."

"That must have been some wet dream, if you're not worried about getting sunburned. You always worry about sunscreen."

Emma turned over and then adjusted the lounge.

Tina could tell she was avoiding eye contact. *It must have been a wet dream! Good for her!*

"No, I'm not worried about anything right this second. I'm on vacation and I'm still half asleep." Emma adjusted her sunglasses. "I hardly closed my eyes last night."

"Reliving the moment, I'll bet." Tina grinned. She was proud of her friend and not because she'd picked up some guy. No, it was because Emma had guts. She just kept her standards so high she couldn't always meet them. For some reason Emma felt she was average, but she was in fact exceptional. Point in case, she was the only secretary willing to take on extra duties, like the new computer program. "I'll bet Melissa's gnashing her teeth right now because you aren't there to keep her organized."

"She's organized, terrifyingly organized. She reminds me of my old high-school principal when she looks at me over the top of those glasses. I always have trouble saying no to her." She shrugged. "But she usually has my best interest at heart."

"You mean the best interest of the firm. It's your own sense of loyalty that you see reflected in Melissa's glasses. That's why you keep hanging on when you really want to move on."

Emma yawned. "Could be. I do seem to be in a holding pattern and I'd like to think it's due to loyalty and not laziness but I really don't want to talk about work."

"How about describing that dream?"

Emma smirked. "No such luck. Tell me about the club."

Tina barely resisted teasing her friend for the scalding blush on her face, which was very much at odds with her nonchalant attitude. "The club's nice and the Italian safety officer dances like he's taken lessons. When he whispers in my ear in Italian, I practically melt."

"Andres speaks Spanish—at least I think that's what it was from what little I remember from my three years of high-school Spanish."

"You should have asked him for a translation."

"He made me too happy to care." Emma smiled.

Tina adjusted her teeny-tiny bikini top. "Now that you've gotten the one-night-stand thing out of your system you might try concentrating on one guy. Take things a little slower. After all, it's supposed to be a vacation." Tina knew Emma would be happier with one guy than going from man to man just to prove that she could.

"I'm not sure I can look at another man just yet."

Tina immediately straightened up. "You couldn't have let yourself get that hooked on him."

"I'm okay, Counselor. I just meant that I need a little breathing room."

"Okay. It's just that I want you to have fun, even if you can't help comparing every guy on the cruise to Andres. I want you to get your money's worth." Tina flicked her hair back over her shoulder.

"It's already been worth both the time and money. Andres was wonderful."

Tina watched her friend stroke her chin. Tina could only imagine what Emma was thinking about but it was probably in opposition to Emma's overall goals for the cruise. "He's miles away. Let him go. What you need is someone *on* the cruise. Not some fantasy man. Believe me. No man, no matter how yummy, is perfect."

"I don't know. I think I know which lawyer you were talking about last night. It's gotta be Tyler Walden. He's the only man you mention in that offhand way. And he's the total package—gorgeous, rich and successful."

"I would never talk about Tyler in any special way." But Tina nibbled on her thumbnail, which totally irritated her because it was one of the many nervous habits she'd worked hard to break. "Tyler doesn't interest me in the least."

"Well, this is the time to snag him. You look pretty fab in that tiny red suit."

"*You* look great. And you'd see all the looks guys are tossing your way if you paid attention."

"I don't see anything," she lied.

Tina sighed. "Guys are spoiled these days. They expect a woman to give them an opening that's so obvious, it's pathetic. In fact, the more I think of it the more I agree with your assessment about dating being like job interviews. It *is* work." Tina leaned back in her chair.

Frowning, Emma asked, "When did the dating game get to be like a bad reality show with women falling all over themselves to get the guy interested?"

Fighting a grin, Tina said, "It's because there are more available women than men. And all of those available women have a stigma about being single. It makes them seem pathetic. And pathetic is the kiss of death." She flicked a hand. "And the men out there aren't worth the trouble anyway."

"Is that why you refuse to go out with Tyler? Because you're afraid he'll disappoint you?"

Tina grimaced and just caught herself before she put another manicured nail into her mouth for a nibble.

When had that nasty nervous habit come back?

"Of course he'll disappoint me. And I have a rule about dating other lawyers. In fact I have a rule against any kind of serious dating. It's too distracting and leads to relationships, which have a tendency to take time and effort away from the really important things, like your career or school."

"Even if I get to school, I don't want to skip the fun part of life—I think I want it all." Emma sounded a little tentative.

"Why bother? Once you get married the romance goes away."

"A little cynical, are we?"

Tina pushed her hair back again. "They don't call me The Shark for nothing. Of course I'm cynical."

"It's not about being The Shark," Emma said more gently. "I'm guessing it's all about the foster homes you grew up in."

This time Tina did nibble on her nail, just the corner where it felt rough. Where the hell was a nail file when you needed one? "I wish I'd never told you that story."

"I know you want children."

Tina shrugged. "When I'm ready for a baby I'm going down to the local sperm bank to select a father for my child. That way I won't have to worry about visitation, child support or a deadbeat dad."

Emma just looked at her. "I guess this is how we balance each other out."

Tina put her hand up to her sunglasses to make a point. "How is it that you're still wearing those rose-colored glasses? What about your parents?"

Emma sighed. "Yes, but it doesn't cancel out what they shared with me and with each other over the years."

"It's got to be the fling you had last night. You've still got stars in your eyes," Tina told her tartly, and then softened her voice to add, "But you're right. That's what I like about you. You manage to be practical and still have faith. Some days I'd give anything to have a bit of faith in the decent human values I see trampled every day in court. Hell, I'd settle for people being civil to each other."

"What are you doing on a singles' cruise if you don't hope to meet someone nice?"

Tina shrugged. "I hope to meet someone nice, just so it's nice *and* short. I even did a little homework. It seems the cruises attract busy, successful people who don't have much time to date—as well as the losers, desperate and depressed," Tina added feeling silly for admitting she'd actually done research.

"What? Did the research use the words '*losers, desperate and depressed*'?" Emma laughed.

"Not exactly. But it was definitely implied."

Emma strained her neck to look at something.

Tina turned to see what had attracted Emma's attention. "Oh." She sighed. "There's something so erotic about watching a person shower in public." Tina watched avidly. "I definitely should go and talk to him—offer him a towel or a massage."

"Forget him and focus on Tyler. You have so much in common with him—more than the Italian safety officer or the hunk in the shower. You're on vacation so you could ignore your rules and give him a try."

A waiter came by and Tina signaled him decisively. "The special. And make it a double, please."

The waiter grinned and then turned around and headed for the bar.

"Why are you challenging me when I'm on vacation?" Tina complained.

"Because you made me stretch my horizons and I got to meet Andres. I already feel like I'm a bolder, more adventurous Emma. I set a goal and I've already accomplished some of the things I wanted to do. It's amazing," Emma gushed. "And I just want you to have an equally amazing time on this cruise."

Tina took off her glasses. "Tyler is not one to mess with. Trust me. Even a fling with him would be complicated and stressful."

"In the long run it might be more fun than going to a sperm bank."

"What if I promise to have a drink with him? Is that going to satisfy you?"

"Yes. If he's half the man I've heard he is then he'll do the rest."

"So I have a drink with Tyler and you look around for another hunk. But take it easy. I don't want you to get hurt and I don't think this one-night-stand thing is your style—though I certainly admire you for giving it your all. I'm going to buy you a henna tattoo in Key West to celebrate. Something daring."

"Okay." Emma's face lit up. "I've always wanted a tattoo…at least a henna one. Too bad I can't show it off to Andres."

Tina put her glasses back on, hoping to hide her concern. "Put some sunscreen on. Those stars in your eyes are giving off so much light you're going to get burned," she warned, unable to keep all of the worry from her voice.

"You are a very good friend, you know that?"

Tina was glad she had her sunglasses on. It always took her by surprise when Emma went mushy on her. "I'm not. I'm a bitch. The Shark. And don't you forget it because occasionally I do bite."

"Not without cause. You hide your soft center."

"Stop. You make me sound like a piece of chocolate." Tina waved her off and then watched as Emma sat back with a sigh. *This could be worse than the thing with Brad. I hope she's not getting her soft heart broken all over again.*

5

THE MUSIC PULSATED. Emma gyrated. The man smiled and she tried to smile back as the long strands of hair flopped over his bald spot. Two drinks since her nap and this guy still didn't look good. Emma couldn't seem to get rid of Jim the loser.

Out of the corner of her eye she caught sight of a tall dark man. She jerked around trying to see him more clearly. All evening long she'd been catching glimpses of Andres. Either it was just wishful thinking or a crazy remnant of the dream from this morning—she didn't know which.

"I'm going to sit down for a while," she shouted.

"Can I get you something to drink?"

"No, I'll be fine." Emma walked towards where Tina was sitting as fast as she could without offending Jim. The club decor included artistic cement palm trees climbing the walls in three dimensions. Their table was tucked under a huge trunk and behind them was a wall painting of sailing boats embedded with tiny sparkling lights. Behind other tables were pictures of beach bonfires and more sparkling lights. A huge golden moon hung above the dance floor.

"Save me," Emma begged Tina as she scooted into the cozy booth.

Tina nodded. "You got it." Then she turned her most dazzling smile on Jim, who was breathing like a freight train as he approached their table. "Jim, would you mind if we have a chance for a little girl talk? Just for a while?"

"Do you want me to go get you a drink?"

"No."

"Not even water?"

"No, just some privacy, please."

He nodded dumbly and headed for the bar.

"Thank you. I swear the guy breathes like he hasn't worked out in years. I'm afraid he's going to have a heart attack out on the dance floor."

"Come on, you're just afraid you might have to do CPR on the guy."

"Desperately afraid!" Emma took a sip of her water. "Why do I end up with the terminally bald and you get the safety officer? He's definitely prime. Doesn't he have any cute friends?"

"Sure. I'll ask. Oh shit." Tina looked down at her nails.

Emma smiled. Only one person on this ship could make Tina lose her cool. "It must be the lawyer."

"No, it's this nail."

But Emma saw him, leaning on the bar oozing perfect lawyer confidence from every pore. This man was even good enough for Tina. "Yeah, right, so why is he looking right at you?"

"He's just trying to irritate me."

Tina did the unthinkable. She put the newly manicured, gold-inlaid nail in her mouth and began to nibble on it. In fact, the usually formidable woman looked so vulnerable Emma couldn't help but be intrigued. "He's definitely trying to irritate you. How dare he hang out at the bar on a singles' cruise," she teased.

"Yeah, what's a guy like Tyler doing trolling on a cruise ship anyway? He can have any woman he wants. All he has to do is whistle or something." Tina took a sip of her drink and then stirred it around and around.

"You did the research. He's a busy guy who doesn't have time to look for women."

"And if you're that gullible then you belong on a jury, preferably one of mine."

Emma smiled. "Tina, I'd say you were interested in Tyler."

"I don't date lawyers. Men don't like it when you're in competition with them." She put the drink down abruptly. "And he's not interested anyway."

"Yeah, right. And he's also not looking this way."

"He's not." But Tina definitely seemed distracted.

Emma thought Tina might need a catalyst. "I wonder if he's a good dancer."

"Probably not. He'll just *think* he's a good dancer."

"I think I'll ask him to dance anyway. Then you'll know. Maybe he's taken Salsa lessons, too. He might have great moves," she teased, "on the dance floor and off."

Tina smirked. "You're going to ask him to dance?"

"Think of it as one of my cruise challenges. I need to do something exciting every day. Remember, I'm stretching my horizons."

Tina nodded. "And doing a good job, but this isn't necessary. It's dangerous. Tyler is no one to play with."

"Why should I settle for Jim with the three strands of hair, when I can hit on a gorgeous lawyer?"

"He's not gorgeous."

"He's definitely gorgeous."

Tina took her nail out of her mouth and then tapped it on the table. "You don't have the guts to ask him to dance."

"I do. I have enough courage in me to do almost anything. I've been using your techniques and so far they're working out perfectly. I just keep thinking about the way Andres responded to me. Gives me all kinds of confidence."

"He's not going to be interested in either one of us."

That certainly didn't sound like Tina, which gave Emma hope that she was right about her friend's interest in Tyler. "First let's find out if he can dance or you'll be bored after five minutes." Emma pushed her hair back and finished off a bottle of water instead of her drink. "Asking a man to dance should be simple. I'll just smile a lot and wiggle my hips and he'll be following me around like a puppy for the rest of the night. And if I have to do CPR on him it'll be my pleasure."

"This I've got to see. I'll bet you a massage that you cave in before you ever get the words out of your mouth." Tina's expression turned genuine. "Just remember if you get up there and you can't speak to him, you can order another drink. I don't want you to be embarrassed."

Did Tina sound just a bit wistful?

"Don't worry about me," Emma said, taking Tina's

hand. She could feel the ragged nail under her finger. "I'm going to do this because I'd be crazy to turn down a massage and also because I want to know if I have the guts. But I'm not poaching. He's definitely for you. I'm just going to lure him over here so the two of you can talk."

Tina didn't give an inch. Instead she put on her inscrutable lawyer face. "I'm not interested. You're welcome to him. I don't date lawyers. Men get weird about competition no matter how much they protest that it's not going to be a problem."

"I think you protest a bit too much, girlfriend."

"And I think you're procrastinating, girlfriend. Because there's no way you're up for it. Not that I care either way."

The butterflies in Emma's stomach fluttered up into her throat and she couldn't seem to get up out of her seat.

Then Tina nibbled her nail, which gave Emma the incentive to grab the drink in front of Tina and slug it down.

But did she need liquid courage?

Wasn't she the girl who'd been with Andres last night? The girl who'd blossomed because of his attention? She'd learned so much about herself and that sometimes taking a chance could be the most rewarding, most important thing a woman could do for herself.

She put the drink down with a flourish and winked at Tina.

She rose to her feet and sashayed over to the bar where Tyler Walden rested against the wood as if he owned the place. Carefully cut blond hair emphasized his face and his laser-blue eyes assessed her before she ever reached him. Normally, Emma would have turned and run away from a man this beautiful, but tonight she didn't care if the big-shot lawyer said yes or no.

Andres had told her that she was beautiful. And for some reason she actually felt beautiful. This heady feeling of self-worth just seemed to come naturally.

"Hi. I wondered if you'd dance with me. I've been stuck with the balding guy all night and I wanted a change of pace." She even held out her hand. "I'm Emma."

"I'm Tyler Walden and I'd love to dance with you."

Emma's spirit soared. She'd approached an attractive, successful lawyer and he'd said yes. *You did it, girlfriend! Now the sky's the limit.*

Tyler put a guiding hand on her shoulder and they headed out onto the floor. The music changed to a slow song so he pulled her in close. He danced well. They moved smoothly around the floor. Emma wished she'd met Tyler before she'd met Andres; maybe there would have been more chemistry between them. Then she caught sight of Tina gnawing on another nail and she was glad there was very little chemistry.

The song ended and the two of them stood awkwardly for a moment. "Would you like to join my friend and me?" Emma offered.

Tyler's quick glance at the table convinced Emma. He was definitely interested in Tina. His immediate nod confirmed her suspicion. They headed for the table and Tina whipped her nail out of her mouth and straightened up into her usual sophisticated posture.

"Hello, Tyler. What are *you* doing on a singles' cruise?" Tina asked the question as if she was interrogating a witness.

"Probably the same thing you are, Counselor."

"Call her Tina," Emma said, grinning inside at the lethal look Tina sent her. "She's harmless after a few drinks."

Tyler looked at Tina. "I doubt she's been harmless a moment in her life." Then he turned to Emma. "Are you an attorney?"

Emma shook her head. "I'm an assistant at a law firm."

Tyler rubbed his hands together. "Well, you should have seen Tina in court a few months ago. She dominated. I felt for Dominic Sanchez—he's with our firm."

"I'll bet she's tough in court. But she's really nice in person," Emma said.

Tina remained stubbornly silent with a grim little smile fixed on her face.

Tyler just looked as though he didn't know what to contribute.

"Well, what interesting cases are you working on at the moment?" Emma prompted Tyler.

"Well, I've a full caseload but there's one case with the potential to help create new law. We intend to pursue this with a much higher court."

"I'd like to hear about it," Tina said offhandedly.

"Now here's the real challenge," Tyler began.

Emma felt herself beginning to nod off as the conversation turned to lawyer lingo, so she excused herself and headed up on deck to clear her head.

Leaning over the chest-high rail, she enjoyed the view. The sea looked beautiful under the almost-full moon, and the wind blew her tousled hair around her face.

So far she hadn't seen anyone interesting. In fact, she wondered where was a bold, exotic man who could sweep a woman off her feet while whispering love words into her ear on a moonlight beach? The kind of man who would push a thong out of the way to pleasure a woman and then casually tuck that same thong into his pocket as a trophy?

The kind of man who wasn't on the ship anymore.

"Who are you dreaming of out here in the moonlight?" His deep voice came out of her dreams and into reality. "You still remind me of a mythical creature, a siren, here to entangle me in your charms."

Emma turned, not believing it was Andres. "I was dreaming of a man and a beautiful moonlit beach."

"I dreamed of you, too."

"Andres?" Could he be real? His eyes were as mysterious as the shadows, and his smile gleamed.

Emma leaned forward and touched his arm. *He's real.* "What are you doing here?" She knew she sounded accusatory, surprised and almost frightened. She stepped back as all of those things mixed with the heat she felt just being within a few feet of him. "Maybe, I've had too much to drink." She raised her hand to her spinning head. She'd been trying to get used to the idea that she would never see him again and here he was.

"I've missed you, Emma."

"I thought you lived on Grand Bahama."

"I didn't say that. You assumed and you seemed so enamored with the thought that I couldn't bear to disappoint you."

"You've been on the ship? I *thought* I saw you in the club."

"I've been here all along. But I didn't know how to admit it to you. I was afraid you'd be too angry to speak to me."

Oh my gosh, the things I let him do to me on the beach. She blushed. "I *am* angry at you. You lied to me."

"Not really."

"And I told you about my fantasies and you did that thing with the milkshake." She put her hands on her hot cheeks. "I can't believe I…but I never expected to see you again."

"I told you about my fantasies as well and then I spent today debating whether or not I should approach you. I finally decided that I couldn't resist you for the entire cruise no matter how embarrassed I was by my deception. I wanted to be with you."

"I thought I wanted to be with you, too." She knew she sounded sharp.

He ran a hand through his hair, looking sheepish. "I thought it might be mutual. I hoped you'd forgive me though I know I don't deserve it."

His hair fell softly around his face and she longed to run her hands through it. He had such an effect on her. *Do I chase him off or do I wait and see what develops?* "I still can't believe you're on the ship."

"What can I do to make up for my deception?"

All kinds of things occurred to her. She wanted to be hot and sweaty in his arms. He could tie her up… "I want to…" Her face flamed and so did her temper at the thought of telling him that she wanted to play pirate. What would he think of her?

"When I saw you dancing with that blond man, I felt

so jealous. I had to speak to you, no matter that you might be too angry to forgive me."

"You spied on me!"

"I watched over you."

Had he been watching her when she'd had the wet dream about him? The blush spread to her neck. With Andres on the cruise they could do some of those naughty things she'd been imagining.

"Could you forgive me, *chula*? Give me a break and spend just a little time with me? I won't expect anything physical if you would rather not." He put his arm tentatively around her shoulders.

Emma wanted to pull away from him, but she couldn't imagine letting him go when her body burned for his touch. "I shouldn't forgive you…for wasting an entire day."

He smiled. Then he raised her hand to his face and gently, seductively, kissed her knuckles. "I'll have to make it up to you."

"I've missed you."

"*Chula*, you're all I can think about."

She desperately wanted to have his hands on her. But she needed to *think*. "I want to do everything…" she tried to follow her own train of thought, but all she could do was feel how close he was, how warm, and how she'd been missing him in the cool wind when she'd thought he was so far away. "The milkshake thing and definitely the thong thing."

He laughed softly and guided her backwards until he'd trapped her gently against the side of the ship with his hips and shoulders. Emma leaned into the sweet pressure of his arousal. He nipped her ear gently as his fingers followed the deep neckline of her dress. Angling her away from the view of anyone coming towards the railing and shielding her with his body, he pushed the top of her dress down far enough to capture her nipple between his fingers.

Emma could have sworn his touch turned her brain off and turbo-charged her libido.

"I would love to make love to you, *corazonsito*. In whatever way would please you the most. I have a private cabin if you'd like to accompany me there." He rolled her nipple around in his fingers with just the perfect amount of pressure.

She gulped down a gasp, took a deep breath of the fresh air, and tried to gather her scattered thoughts.

As if he sensed her hesitation he leaned down to take her naked nipple in his mouth and suckle her. This time she did gasp.

When he came up for air so did Emma. "I would love to go to your room," she gasped. "Do we need to stop at my cabin and get the condoms? We have some that glow in the dark." Emma was proud she'd remembered to protect herself in spite of Andres's heady lovemaking to distract her.

"What game do you imagine playing with those condoms?" He wrapped his arm around her and drew her face intimately close as if encouraging her to tell her secrets.

She could feel herself melting against him. "I imagine you naked in the hot tub under the stars wearing only a condom to light my way," she said it in a hushed whisper, embarrassed by her ridiculous fantasy.

He leaned forward and placed a sweet, gentle kiss on her lips. "Tell me about another fantasy. One we can work on tonight."

The world spun as she thought of all the things he could do for her, in a cabin all night long. And what about the bondage thing? Would he be interested in a pirate scenario?

"You can make everything up to me by playing pirate. I really do like the idea of bondage—gentle bondage." She gulped the sea air.

"I would love to make every one of your fantasies come true." He ran his fingers over her face in a tentative, tender way.

"You make me feel like I'm finally fully alive." She pressed against him. "Wow," she said. "This pirate has a sword."

He laughed. "I certainly do." He gently pushed her dress back into place and then took her by the hand to propel her along the deck towards one of the side entrances.

"My cabin isn't this way," she protested a few minutes later in the elevator.

"I have what we need, Emma. I'll take care of you, *chula*. Don't be afraid."

"Okay."

He leaned in, pushing her against the elevator wall. She could feel every inch of his firm body.

"It would be my pleasure to take care of you." His whiskey voice flowed over her as he nibbled on her ear. "I'll fulfill your every dream."

His fingers traveled down her neck toward her neckline.

Her heart rate went up. She licked her lips, tilted her head up and gazed into those dark eyes.

"I love it when you look at me like that."

"Like what?" Her voice rose a little.

"Like you did on the beach, your eyes huge and hungry."

She really wanted to be kissed, cuddled and made love to right there in the elevator, but they'd already arrived at his floor. He gave her a little shove and she obediently went along as he guided her down the long corridor to his stateroom.

"I'm glad you have a private cabin. My roommate will likely be home tonight."

He stopped at the door to a cabin and got out his plastic key card. "You won't have to go back. You can sleep in my arms tonight."

Emma sighed.

He lifted his face. His eyes were mysterious in the dim light. "Is that a yes?" The door swung open.

"As long as you don't disappear again," she half teased, looking inside the stateroom, which didn't appear much different from hers except he had a queen-size bunk.

He touched her face. "I wouldn't dream of it. This night is about you and fulfilling your needs, Now, maybe you want me to order you something from room service?"

"Maybe you should just sweep me up in your arms and have your way with me." She leaned against him and whispered, "Pirate sex."

He grinned, a lecherous grin that shook her a little. After all what did she know about the man? Emma's feet seemed to stick at the threshold of his stateroom. How could she have felt so eager a few minutes ago and suddenly be scared to death? "Maybe I've had too much to drink after all," she fibbed.

He stroked the side of her face with such tenderness it weakened her.

"Don't be afraid, Emma. After all, a cruise is all about fantasy. I only want to please you."

"Are you sure this is a good idea?"

He pulled her into the room, and then before she could protest, he bent down and threw her over his shoulder exactly like pirate booty.

Emma couldn't breathe to protest. *How dare he manhandle her!*

"Put me down." It didn't come out as loudly as she would have liked, but at least he knew she didn't like this caveman stuff.

Instead of putting her down, he patted her bottom. And he didn't stop. He rubbed and petted, creating clever little tendrils of sensation that kept her from wriggling in protest.

What if his fingers moved up under the skirt?

As if he could read her dirty little mind, Andres slipped his hand under the fabric. Emma tried to breathe, but all she could do was gasp as he explored all along the edges of her thong. She shivered. Could she have an orgasm hanging upside down?

It appeared she could; as he slid his fingers in the wet heat he'd discovered he wandered over the territory of her flesh.

"Well, it seems that my sweet captive misspoke." He

dipped deeper. "I think I've discovered how much you do like to be 'manhandled.'"

Emma moaned as he found the perfect spot.

"But you'll have to tell me what you want."

His fingers stroked and teased. Emma closed her eyes, quivering, on the edge, and then he moved those magical fingers away.

"No," she protested. "Don't stop."

"A captive begs for what she wants." He squeezed her butt cheek.

"Please," she breathed.

He stroked her along the edge of the thong, just beyond the place she craved for him to be. Then he cupped her heat with his large hand. All Emma could think of was those fingers and how good they would feel deep inside her. "Please, touch me. Deeper, Andres."

But he let go of her vulnerable flesh. Then he gently lowered her to the bed. Lying on her back, Emma looked up at him. He looked so incredible. "That was amazing," she admitted shyly.

"There is much, much more, my little love captive."

She watched as he hunted around in his suitcase. "What are you going to do?"

"I'm going to leave these sexy heels on your feet and tie your long lush legs together with one of my ties." He took out a red silk tie.

Emma knew he'd probably intended to wear the tie to the captain's reception. "That's silk and if you knot it, you might ruin it."

"Don't worry, *corazon*, it'll be worth ruining it to see it tied around your beautiful legs."

He lifted her legs where they hung off the edge of the bed, and then he tied them together in a surprisingly tight, but not uncomfortable knot.

"That's a sailing knot, very useful to a wicked pirate." Casually he stretched out beside her on the bed as if he tied women up all the time. "In just a minute I may tie your hands."

Emma shuddered as his hands wandered up over her legs, to her thighs, and then he flipped up the edge of her skirt. And she wished a naughty thing. She wished for a mirror above the bed as he lifted her skirt. How did she look, tied, vulnerable with only the thong to cover her? Did she look as sexy as she felt?

"Yes, tie my hands, please." Emma blushed at her blurted request but she trembled with anticipation. "Can you sail?" she asked, thinking of what he'd just said about the knot.

Andres got up and got another tie, royal blue this time. "No, but I've always wanted to. I think I'd love being at sea with its endless horizon. I could look out over the ocean all day long."

Like her, he seemed to desire a life with fewer boundaries. Were his boundaries as self-imposed as her own? she wondered. Could she help to free him as he'd helped her?

He certainly seemed sure of himself as he pinned her hands together up by the pillows. His body was heavy and fully aroused against hers. When he wrapped the tie loosely around her wrists, the heat between her legs intensified to an almost unbearable ache. She rubbed against him, swallowing the plea for him to make love to her right away.

"Are you comfortable?" His voice was hoarse.

It seemed so sweet, that he asked about her comfort. The ties were just symbolic, but whether it was his tenderness or the bondage game, it was entirely effective; she'd never been so aroused. Emma arched against him.

"Be patient, my little prisoner. I don't want to have to beat you," he teased.

"I'll cooperate," she breathed. But she trusted him enough to wonder what a gentle spanking might feel like.

"Good girl." He looked down at her. "What should I do to you first?"

"Anything." And she meant it. She would surely go up in flames no matter where he touched her first.

"I don't know if I'm going to kiss you. I think I'll torture you until you beg for mercy."

Emma shivered, anticipating.

He moved off her and she immediately missed his weight. Slowly, he moved down towards her legs, running his hands over her ankles, calves and thighs. Then his hand crept up under her skirt, running over the curve of her ass. He pulled the material up out of the way to nuzzle her flesh. His tongue slid to the edge of the thong.

Emma lifted her hips to give him better access, almost sobbing with need. Andres pushed her legs further apart, nudging the thong aside to tease her clit with his tongue.

The need grew as he tasted and teased her damp flesh.

"Oh, Andres, please."

He pulled away and blew on the sensitized flesh.

She writhed under him. "Please, Andres. I don't want to play anymore. Please just love me."

He finally thrust his fingers inside her, filling her. Emma tried to reach for his shoulders, but she couldn't use her hands. She must have made a frustrated noise because he came to her, kissing her, opening his mouth to take her in a scorching kiss.

The taste of her own essence on his lips made her feel wickedly erotic. His fingers thrust harder, finally filling her deep desperate need.

"Andres, yes!" she cried out.

His words were a mixture of Spanish and English that made everything seem dreamlike and wonderful all at the same time.

Afterward she lay sated with the intensity of her response. When she opened her eyes it was to his gaze. He hovered directly above her and the golden halo in those brown eyes didn't look angelic—no, he looked devilishly satisfied.

"What?" she asked. "What are you thinking?"

"I'm thinking that I can't allow those beautiful eyes to influence me. I have to remember that I'm an evil pirate."

She licked her lips. "I don't know much about pirates, but it seems to me that a pirate intent on taking advantage of his captive wouldn't wear so many clothes, except maybe his boots, his shark-tooth necklace and a couple of tattoos."

"And what about the hair and the eyeliner?" He leered at her in a horrible impersonation of Johnny Depp in *Pirates of the Caribbean*.

"You'd better work on that pirate voice."

"You don't have the properly respectful attitude. I may have to beat you." He rubbed his hands together and his grin reflected little-boy delight, as though he'd been waiting his entire life to play pirate with her. He pulled the shirt over his head, unzipped his trousers and let them slip down to the floor.

As he untangled his pants from around his ankles, Emma bit her lip to keep from giggling. He was absolutely wonderful and she couldn't wait for her turn to tie him up and nibble all the way from that smile downward.

As soon as she got her energy back. Luxuriously, she stretched.

He watched avidly.

The tie made it awkward but she ran the fingers of one hand through the black hair on his chest. And then lower to the narrow arrow of hair disappearing into his boxer shorts. Bracing herself, she nibbled his nipple.

Andres pushed closer to her. He was incredibly aroused. For a second they just pressed against each other, anticipating the moment to come.

Pushing away from him, Emma slipped one hand awkwardly inside the waistband of the boxers. "If you untie me I'll touch you."

"It'd be my pleasure." He rushed to loosen the knot.

Then she happily pushed his boxer shorts down out of her way, slipping her fingers over his engorged penis. She bent to kiss the velvet flesh and smiled wickedly when Andres sucked in his breath.

She ran her fingers over his balls, soft and vulnerable compared to the rod above. She kissed and licked, hungry to touch him in a way she'd never been hungry to touch a man before.

He grabbed her hands and leaned down over her,

pushing her hands up over her head. With one hand he held her down and with the other he stroked her between the legs.

"I should tie your legs apart so I can ravish you."

Emma just nodded, pushing against the delicious pressure of his fingers.

He began to unravel the tie where it bound her feet.

Reaching for him, she was surprised when he stopped her.

"Raise your arms and put them on the pillows. I love the way it makes your breasts look so full and gorgeous, like they're a feast, an offering." She obediently raised her arms.

He bent down and suckled her.

Emma didn't move as he feasted on her flesh, quivering with pleasure.

"I like having you at my mercy." He stood up and slipped out of his boxers. Emma watched. He looked so good. So incredibly male.

She watched him kneel down at the edge of the bed to untie her legs and then he opened them wide. She felt vulnerable.

Incredibly vulnerable.

She started to put her hand down to cover herself but he stopped her with a shake of his head.

"I said to put your hands up."

Did he sound just a little menacing as he rolled on the condom?

She shivered, wishing for that mirror. How did she look with her hands above her head and her legs spread open?

"There's nothing here to tie your legs to, but you're going to keep them open for me. Aren't you, *chula?*"

He grabbed her ankles and pulled her legs straight up from the bed. Emma wriggled, but he didn't let go. Instead he brought her to the very edge where he fit his penis up against her, while sliding his hands up to her knees.

Emma tried to shift her legs, at least a little, but he pulled her thighs open again.

"You can't move them," he insisted.

She wriggled, feeling as if she might fall off the bed. But then his shaft penetrated her and she forgot all about her legs and feeling vulnerable. She pushed closer to his body.

"Do you like that, *chulita?* All you have to do is scoot as close as you can. Open up for me, petite, and I'll give you everything you want." He stood arrogantly before her prone body, piercing, stabbing, at the heart of her.

She thrust back, pushing against him, gasping, almost sobbing, absorbing his passionate thrusts as he slid yet deeper inside her, filling her completely. She moaned and writhed as he touched every nerve.

With each thrust he brought her closer to what she craved until she began to shudder and he cried out, and they crested in an incredible wave of pleasure.

That wave crested again and again that magical night until Emma finally fell into an exhausted sleep in Andres's arms.

6

ANDRES STOOD over her lounge chair as if captivated by her teensy-weensy thong, and this time she wasn't dreaming. Squelching the familiar urge to pull at the thong, Emma smiled up at him. "Aren't you going to join me?"

"You couldn't keep me away unless you tied me up in my cabin." He winked.

Emma blushed.

He laid his magazine down on the little table beside the lounge chair. "I'm so glad to be here with you. Yesterday I felt like a voyeur, hanging out on the deck above this one and watching you rub sunscreen on your as…body. Looking down on you I thought *que chula nalgitas.*"

Was he blushing as he spread his towel down? He was so cute. "What does that mean? Is it Spanish?"

"Roughly translated, that sophisticated Spanish phrase means 'What a butt.' We used to say it as kids in my grandmother's neighborhood."

"Well, thank you. But I have my doubts any man could be thinking that in English or Spanish."

"Are you kidding? I'd have to kill any guy who dared think that about you." His deep voice mesmerized her. But somehow he almost sounded familiar…

She shook her head. His rough sexy voice made it difficult to concentrate on anything but her wish to drag him back to his stateroom. He'd be so great at phone sex. He's probably great at any kind of sex. But there's something…

A waiter showed up with two coffee cups and interrupted her train of thought. He smiled and held them up. Andres signed the ticket, thanked the waiter and then took the cups. He held them out to Emma. "Regular or latte? I didn't know which one you'd prefer."

"Oh I'd love the latte. You *are* wonderful. I desperately need caffeine—you kept me up too late."

"I'm hoping some caffeine and a nap will rejuvenate both of us. I guess I should be sorry that I wore you out."

She smiled. "I'm expecting you to make it up to me."

"I'd love to." His gaze touched her.

She suddenly felt as if she was wearing less than a thong.

He held up his coffee cup. "Here's to new adventures." They clinked their cups.

"So tell me more about what your plans are for changing your life."

"Maybe paralegal school in the fall. But…" She stopped, unable to give him her standard evasive answer. What if he reacted like Brad? Instead Emma held up her hand. "Wait. Do you mind if we don't do this?"

"What? Get to know each other?" He took a sip of his coffee.

"Yeah. Let's skip the interview part. Okay? We'll just be a couple of strangers who have an instant sexual attraction and leave it that way. It goes better with the fantasy."

"It doesn't bother you, not knowing anything at all about one another?"

Did he look relieved?

"What's the difference? What're the odds we're ever going to see each other again? Let's just fly by the seat of our pants." She could feel a devilish smile spreading across her face. Somehow this plan was working. The game went on and it was turning out to be so much more enjoyable than she'd ever dreamed.

He looked at her with a dark fathomless gaze. "What if I knew something about you—what if I felt like I knew a lot about you? What if I'd come a long way to be with you?"

Boy, he was really good at sounding sincere when he was giving a standard line of bull.

She pushed her hair back from her face, again enjoying its straightened texture. "I don't want to know anything. Next thing you know we'll have turned this into a relationship interview. Then you'll run away because you feel crowded and I'll get upset because I can't keep your interest."

He shrugged. "Okay, *hermosa,* we won't ask a bunch of personal questions. Instead, maybe we should discuss our itinerary for the next few days."

"That sounds good." She sipped her latte. "What's *hermosa* mean?"

"It means beautiful or gorgeous."

"And *chula?*"

"About the same."

"I like those exotic words."

"I'm glad, because they suit you."

"Remember, you don't know anything about me."

"I know that I shouldn't have let my sassy captive leave the cabin."

She lifted her sunglasses to smile boldly at him. "Good idea."

She put her glasses into place and thought about how it felt when he touched her. The silence lengthened. He stretched out and closed his eyes as if he were going to tan or sleep.

Emma shifted in the lounge chair, aroused.

The silence stretched.

Reaching for her latte, she peeked over at him. He lay very still. Was he sleeping or just bored out of his mind? What could she say that would lend itself to the fantasy and not just be tedious? Hadn't she killed any chance of a meaningful conversation with her insistence they abstain from the verbal part of the relationship? Should she simply admit that she was aroused and ask him to take her back to the cabin and take care of her little problem? Wasn't that what every man wanted? A woman who wanted nothing more than his body?

The silence screamed like Emma's nerves. She turned over and this time she couldn't help but tug at her thong. "Why did I wear this thing?" she grumbled under her breath.

"So you'd look beautiful for me."

She looked over into his dark eyes. "I thought I'd bored you to sleep. And why would you assume I need to look beautiful for you? I might be trolling for other men. That man in the shower, maybe." She nodded her head in the direction of the shower. "Yesterday, Tina was commenting on how erotic it is to watch men shower in public."

"Tina is a fascinating woman."

"She's so brave."

"You are also brave."

Did he think she was brave because she'd approached him in that bar? He had no idea how nervous she'd been. "It's just that Tina's not afraid of anything but her own vulnerability. The old fear-itself thing. She's definitely my mentor."

Andres wondered if Emma knew how much of herself she'd already given away. Because of Brad or perhaps a series of poorly chosen boyfriends, she had a bad opinion of dating and men, and she'd chosen a unique way to handle her problem. Instead of retreating, she'd thrown her natural caution to the wind.

"I think I might be burning on my shoulders. Would you check? My skin's so fair, I need to use a lot of sunscreen."

Her tone might have been innocent, but her body language was seductive. He had to admit that both the combination of her innocence of spirit and her desire to explore and develop her sexuality was much more lethal than anything her jaded friend had to offer.

Here was the girl you could take home to your parents and they would never know she was incredible in bed. The best of both worlds, the girl next door and the siren in one damn sexy package.

"Sunscreen? Andres? Can you help me with the sunscreen?"

"Of course I'll rub some sunscreen on your beautiful back if you promise to stop watching the man in the shower."

"I don't know. You sound rather bloodthirsty when you're acting jealous. I kinda like it."

Andres picked up the sunscreen from the little table between their chairs. "I assume this belongs to you since it's UV-30 and you're smart enough to take care of your skin." He admired both her fair skin and her practicality.

"It must be great to have such sunproof skin. It must be your Spanish background."

She sounded so admiring. He'd pulled off the facade, even if he hadn't been much of a gentleman.

Then why was he so anxious to tell her his real name? In this role-playing game he'd done everything right. Yet he desperately wanted to hear her call him Tony.

He wanted to tell her the truth.

"You look so pensive. What are you thinking? Are you tired of playing the pirate?" she teased.

"I'll be your scoundrel, tonight, today, you name it." He gently scooted her over in her lounge chair. "I'm going to get close because I need to be sure I get all of your skin." The truth was that he couldn't wait to touch her again, no matter that he'd held her all night long.

The thought made his hands shake.

He might be getting in too deep. And what was he going to do when she saw him at the office? How could he tell her the truth? She'd forgiven him for not telling her that he was a passenger on the cruise. Would she forgive him as easily the second time he deceived her? Why should she?

I need to tell her the truth.

She stretched against him, lying almost naked beside him, except for the thong and the bikini strap across her back. Temptation warred with his conscience.

He put his hands down on the soft supple skin of her waist because he couldn't help himself. He couldn't walk away from her just yet.

He'd take his chances.

THE SKIN on her waist burned where Andres touched her. Emma had never been so sensitive to a lover's touch. She wanted his hands all over her, but she knew she'd never have the nerve to ask him to rub sunscreen on her butt. She felt her face grow hot at the thought.

"Do you want a sip of the latte?" Andres offered.

"No, I can wait. Your hands are a mess and I'm trying to relax." But she felt wired.

"I promise to make you feel more relaxed."

Not likely.

He put his hands on her shoulders and began to rub.

Her skin rippled in appreciation. A few seconds and she lost herself in the sensation.

"Am I rubbing too hard? I don't want to hurt you."

Emma sighed. "No way, I'm definitely falling in love with your massage technique."

"You're too easy to please. But I'm glad you've forgotten about the man who was in the shower."

"What man?" she asked lazily, half asleep, aroused and totally happy with the results of her bright idea.

"Ah I've captivated you. What else do you like besides back rubs?"

"I love to have my scalp massaged," she murmured.

"Does your boyfriend do it for you?"

She blinked. Was he trying to sneak in a personal question?

"Not today," she protested. "I'm not going to answer any questions. I'm pretending to be a pirate's booty."

"Good. Then we're on the same page." He moved further down on her back.

Basking in the warmth of his touch, she tensed up as he massaged lower and then lower. There. Had his hand slipped into a questionable zone? She sat up and sort of pulled away, only to realize how much of the lounge he took up. "I think that's good. Thank you."

His eyes were deep. He looked as dazed as she felt. Emma signaled the waiter and asked for two specials of the day to cool them both off. At home she would never have considered drinking before noon but she was on vacation with a gorgeous man in tow.

The man in question hovered attentively and, because of their proximity, she couldn't help but notice that he was aroused.

"Um, Andres, could you slide over?"

He moved, almost reluctantly.

She couldn't help feeling womanly and powerful. She'd aroused a sexy man without much effort. What could she do if she pushed it a little?

Andres started to get up from the side of her lounge chair.

She stopped him with a look and a crook of her finger. "Andres, I just need you to make sure you get my, uh, more sensitive areas. It's the first time this year that

I've worn a thong and I wouldn't want to burn my, uh, buns, so do you think you could put more sunscreen on me?" she asked, hoping it sounded provocative.

"Of course, *chula*, I wouldn't want you to burn in any sensitive areas."

She watched avidly as he rubbed more cream on his hands. Then she turned around to look at him as he put those large hands directly in the center of her buttock cheeks and massaged. She closed her eyes, in heaven with the sensation of his hot hands on her cool skin. Or was it her skin burning up under his hands?

Either way it was pure sin. As if they were "doing it" right here on the deck.

"Are you getting hungry? Would you like to have lunch in one of the restaurants? Which one's your favorite?"

How could he concentrate enough to talk? She felt as though her tongue was hanging out. "Uh, I guess the Hula Haven. I like the buffet. It's got lots of fresh stuff and the dark chocolate cheesecake is awesome." She laughed ruefully. "I'm going to have to go on a diet when I get back home."

"And where is home?"

"Jacksonville, Florida." Emma turned around to look at him. "You tricked me!"

He leaned over and kissed her mouth. "I can't help it. I want to know everything about you. And you definitely have no need to diet."

"Where are you from?" she challenged him.

"I'm from Denver."

"Oh." It was so far from Florida. "See, this is meant

to be a fantasy, because we live so far apart from one another. But Denver is nice. I went skiing in Colorado one time," she finished hastily.

"Florida has its attractions." He patted her cheeks and then wiped his hands off with a towel. "Are you getting hungry yet?"

Was it a loaded question? "I'm not sure what you have in mind."

"I just want to be around to help you work off the cheesecake."

Then she'd be sure to eat two pieces.

The waiter brought two specials. Emma handed him her ship's card, grinning at his timing. She took a sip of one of the drinks. Delicious.

She got to her feet with drink in hand.

"Where are you going?"

"We're going." Emma gathered her courage along with her stuff and then looked directly at him. "I like your cabin idea so much I thought we'd get room service and then work it off. Or work it off first. Or maybe forget lunch altogether."

She waited.

Unsure.

She'd never really propositioned a man before, especially not so blatantly. And if he laughed at her or even pretended he wasn't interested she might just die from embarrassment. It would be a million times worse than the thing with Brad.

However, Andres didn't laugh. No, his eyes widened as what she'd suggested registered, and then he practically jumped out of his lounge chair, spilling it and his towel in the process.

Emma giggled happily. Seducing a big, strong, handsome man certainly had its rewards.

EMMA TRIED to be quiet as she packed for the day's adventure but Tina rolled over in her bunk and then sat up, rubbing her sleepy eyes.

"Where are you going?"

"I'm going snorkeling with Andres. It's called the stingray adventure and I didn't tell him that I've never snorkeled before."

Tina looked confused. "Not a good plan. Why not?"

Emma went over to sit on Tina's bunk. "I'm not sure. I guess because I want him to think I'm sophisticated and experienced."

"How in the world are you going to pull it off?"

"Is it that hard?" Emma grimaced. What in the world had she gotten herself into? This was what happened when you didn't think things through a million times.

Tina seemed to consider for a minute. "No. Just watch him carefully, and be sure to seal the mask tightly to your face. Remember to breathe in and out through your mouth. But everyone sputters a few times so if you do it won't be glaringly obvious. I think you're being silly though. He'll feel so big and strong if you let him give you a lesson." She yawned.

"He already knows so much about me—he sneaks questions in when I'm concentrating on other things. I don't want him to find out that I am an ordinary woman without an exciting bone in my body. I just want to keep him interested."

"Honey, you've spent every waking moment with him—he couldn't be more interested. I think you're working too hard. You should relax."

Somewhat reassured, Emma asked, "Is Tyler taking you somewhere today?"

Tina immediately pushed back her hair back. "Only because the man's so irritating and insistent. But I already paid for our little Jet Ski adventure. It's driving him crazy."

Emma walked over to pick up her bag. "You go, girl. Keep driving them crazy. That's my motto for the day."

EMMA WAS DRIVING him crazy, handing him the sunscreen to put on her at every opportunity even as they now stood in two feet of water. He wondered if she knew how much he wanted to slip his hands under her tiny swimsuit and ravage her nipples.

Here they were on an island, surrounded by heavenly views, with snow-white sand and graceful palms, and all he could think about was laying her down and having his way with her.

"You're taking such good care of my skin. I won't even have a tan line when I get home."

"You could lie on the beach naked to avoid tan lines. I can hardly think for imagining you naked." Andres nibbled her neck while letting his slick fingers roam over her stomach, just inside the material of the bikini bottoms.

"Oh, that feels so good." She leaned back against his shoulder. "I wish we were alone so I *could* get naked."

"Too bad you don't need any sunscreen in the cabin.

I'm beginning to think of this as foreplay." He ran his fingers slowly over her slick skin.

"I think you've got me covered." She chuckled.

Some tourists came towards them.

Without a word Emma scooted backwards against him, hiding his erection.

"Thank you, chula."

In the next few minutes the stingray adventurers were broken into small groups and instructed to go to the dock where there was a large wooden box full of fins and masks. "What size do you wear, little one? I'll get them for you."

He could see she was pink with pleasure at his attention.

"Size six, please."

Andres fished the fins out and chuckled as she tried them on, flapping and struggling. He suspected that she'd never snorkeled. He wondered why she wouldn't admit it as they made their way down to the beach.

"This is a cool dose of reality." Emma stood in the waist-deep water. "And I can't see if there are stingrays or not."

You have to put on the mask before you can see anything. But he didn't tease her. It was sweet how she wanted him to think that she was sophisticated and experienced when he was more impressed by her willingness to try everything. Her sweet bravery touched him more than any sophistication ever could.

And her sexuality seared him.

"Visibility gets better out in the lagoon. The water on the beach is full of sand stirred up by the waves."

"Okay." She put on the mask a trifle lopsidedly, looking adorably silly.

"Are there sharks in these waters? I'm not familiar with the area." She wrapped a strand of hair around and around her index finger.

"The water's very warm here so there are fewer types of big sharks. You probably won't see one," he tried to reassure her. The finger thing meant she was nervous. He'd seen it before.

"Wow, I'm disappointed. I love to see sharks. They are so…hungry-looking." Her mask slipped down over one ear as she tried to adjust the straps.

"Can I help you tighten the mask?" He tried not to grab her up and give her a huge hug. She was trying hard to hide her apprehension and it made her so adorable, in a very sexy way.

"It's okay. I've got it. It's just been a while since I've done this."

She leaned over and stroked his arm, giving him a clear view of her breasts. Did she do things like that on purpose to distract him? He was beginning to think she did. Of course, he immediately took advantage of the view.

She struggled, but somehow managed to get everything in place, and then gave him the thumbs-up as she slowly submerged her face. He watched her closely, but the equipment seemed to be working for her.

"Try breathing in."

She came up sputtering. "What?"

"Lie on the surface and then take a shallow breath through your mouth."

"I know how. I'm just rusty and sorta claustrophobic."

Was she actually claustrophobic? He hated being afraid of small spaces. It made him feel helpless and inept. Was that why Emma wouldn't admit she hadn't ever snorkeled before? So she wouldn't feel inept?

He had the feeling her confidence had been shaken by the incident at work. But he had to admire the way she'd come out of hiding. The woman wasn't holding anything back. Nor did he want her to.

He noticed how she crossed her fingers this time before she plunged into the water with a splash. She was definitely gutsy, his Emma. When she didn't come up sputtering, he slipped on his mask and was tempted to cross his own fingers as he followed her.

Andres stayed right behind Emma, distracted by the curves of her body more than anything else. She swam fluidly, beautifully, and the thong left little to his imagination. He wanted to run his hands all over those dangerous curves.

They came to an area about five feet deep and though he saw it coming he couldn't warn Emma without embarrassing her. He watched as she dove down to look at a purplish brain coral and saw her gag through the glass as the mask filled with seawater.

She planted her feet.

He came up next to her.

"Are you okay?" he asked as soon as he slipped out of his mask.

The mask dangled from Emma's hand. "I'm fine." She coughed. "Just got some water in my mouth and nose. This is so fun. I didn't know you could see so much. The water's so clear. But I haven't—" She sneezed and then she coughed. "Seen a ray yet. Have you?"

"Not yet. We probably just have to go out farther. Head out to where the waves are breaking."

Shielding her eyes from the sun, she looked out. "Isn't it dangerous out there in the surf? How can you see anything if it's all stirred up by the waves?"

"We won't go that far but the waves are breaking on coral. If we stay on this side we should be able to see more. Besides that's the way the group went."

"Sorry I'm holding you up. I just like being alone with you." She leaned against him, her skin cool and smooth.

He could hardly breathe for wanting her. Under the waterline he put a familiar hand on her pert ass. "I want to be alone with you, too. But it's probably best to follow the group." He kissed her softly on her salty lips. "Later. I promise I'll make it up to you later."

She smiled crookedly. "Sounds like a plan."

His brave, beautiful girl was amazing and by sharing this experience he suspected they were both getting in beyond their depth. He knew it was dangerous, but he followed her anyway.

After a half hour of weaving their way towards the surf, Emma was getting braver and doing very well. Then a large speckled ray went by and she spun to wave at him and point out the ray. He nodded, watching the ray go by and then looked up to see Emma standing up, or rather trying to stand up, in the water.

Fortunately the water in the lagoon wasn't especially deep. Andres grabbed her shoulders to keep her above the surface; with the swell of the waves, the water here was almost as deep as she was tall. Taking off his mask, he asked, "What happened?"

"I just got excited and went too deep. I should have known better." She coughed deeply.

He grabbed her mask with his other hand from where it lay on the surface of the water. "Are you okay?"

"Yeah, just a mouth full of salt water, nothing to worry about, but I do feel a little queasy."

"Do you want to go back now? I don't mind."

She shook her head firmly. "No. I want to see everything."

"You like it?"

"Yeah, it's great." It came out as a garbled whisper accompanied by more coughing.

"I can see that you think it's great but I think we should go back. I'll give you a back rub and then maybe a front rub."

She took a deep breath. "Not that I don't appreciate your offer, but I want to stay. I mean it. I love the way the rays just seem to fly along the bottom. It's amazing. Plus who knows when I'll get another chance to do this? It's been amazing... I mean, it's been a while."

He even loved that she couldn't lie worth a damn. "You sure you don't want to go back?"

"No. No way. I love this. The water's that true beautiful blue just like in the brochures. And the rays and small fish are fascinating." She grabbed his arm. "Thanks so much for this. I'm having the best time."

"So am I, *querida.*"

He saw her crash and burn a third time. He'd been watching her closely, aware that she'd enthralled him more than the stunning beauty of the sea.

Emma came up this time looking a bit green. "I guess I did it again," she choked out.

"This time it wasn't your fault. It was the dinghy that went by us. It had a wake that washed over your snorkel. It could happen to anyone."

"Thank you."

"For what?"

"For being so nice to me. I know I've held you back. I'm not quite as experienced at this as I pretended." She sneezed forcibly. "And I guess I need to go back now. I feel sick from all of the water I've swallowed."

He put an arm around her shoulders. "It won't take long to wade back to shore. We'll get you some fresh water to rinse out your mouth and you'll feel a whole lot better."

"I hope so," she said doubtfully.

He towed her, enjoying the feel of her pliant body against his.

She drew a deep breath as they walked up out of the water and onto the sand. Then she practically collapsed at his feet in the sand.

"I hope I won't feel so slushy now. It's like there's an ocean rolling around inside my stomach."

"When you're ready to walk we'll get you a drink," Andres said solicitously, knowing that he didn't have a chance of making love with her tonight, and only slightly disappointed. It had been a wonderful day and he was only sorry that she'd gotten seasick.

"I'm sorry if I messed things up." She sounded close to tears. "I so wanted to do this."

He stroked the smooth skin of her face. "You didn't mess things up. You are the most amazing woman. And I'd say that you did it very well indeed."

She smiled and then she grimaced and put a hand on her stomach. "Oh I can't wait to get back on board. Maybe I'll feel better."

Andres smiled. Good thing the ship had stabilizers or she'd likely be sick all night long.

When they got to the ship and disembarked, she turned to Andres and gave him a hug. "That was incredible. Thank you so much. I loved it." She hid her face in the side of his neck. "You smell like the sea."

"I hope that's a compliment."

For a moment she nibbled his skin and he thought maybe she was feeling better. "You even taste like the sea. Another time I'd like to explore this phenomenon but today I don't find the salty taste all that attractive."

"Sorry."

She waved her hand. "No, it's not you."

"Do you want to get changed and go out? There's a great restaurant and bar right here on the dock. I hear the dancing's hot." He ran a finger up her naked arm.

"I would love to." But her smile was forced.

"You should probably nap for a while."

"That sounds heavenly." This time her smile was full of gratitude. "Are you sure you don't mind?"

"No way. I'll just walk you to your cabin and then come back and pick you up in a couple of hours."

She nodded. Then he led her to her cabin. He didn't even get a chance to kiss her at the door; she was in too much of a hurry to get inside and lie down.

A FEW MINUTES later someone knocked at the door. Emma groggily rolled out of bed. Who could it be?

She opened the door to Andres's handsome face. He looked so good, in black slacks and a tropical shirt. "Why are you early?"

"Emma, I'm not early. What's wrong?"

She ran a hand through hair that felt lank from the salt water. "I guess I fell asleep. I'm sorry. I'll be ready in a few minutes."

He took a step inside and then pulled her close. "We don't have to go anywhere, *chulita*. I can come in and we can spend some time together." He nuzzled her neck, his body pressed close.

Emma waited for the flare of desire, but instead her stomach rebelled at the smell of his cologne. She raised a hand to her mouth. "I'm sorry. I think I'm going to be sick." She pushed him out of the cabin door and shut it behind him. Then she just made it to the bathroom in time to be thoroughly sick. The salt water burned even worse coming back up.

She could hear him knocking on the bathroom door, but she didn't let go of the cool base of the toilet.

A few minutes or more later, someone entered the cabin. They opened the door to the bathroom which Emma hadn't taken the time to lock.

"What's wrong with you? Andres grabbed me out of the casino and dragged me up here to check on you. And I left on a lucky streak!" Tina took in the situation and then ran water in the sink. She knelt down to drape a cool, wet hand towel around Emma's forehead.

"I'm sorry. The gallon of salt water I swallowed didn't agree with me."

"How on earth did you manage to swallow enough salt water to make you sick?"

"I kept forgetting. The rays were so great. I just went too deep and then wham! Salt water instead of air. I couldn't control my depth as well as Andres did."

Tina smiled. "I guess you liked the ray encounter."

"I liked it and I think I pulled it off." She took the towel off her forehead and wiped her face with it.

"So you never admitted that you hadn't snorkeled before?"

"No, but I wanted to. I wanted to admit how amazing everything was. But I was afraid he'd think badly of me."

"Why are you so unsure of him?"

"Have you looked at him lately?"

"Have you taken a look at yourself?"

"I'm the same person, only I have straight hair."

"You're amazing. You're brave, sexy and smart. You even got a hint of a tan today. All of the old Emma, with new exciting aspects. Believe me you've got nothing to worry about. You're doing everything you said you would. You're blooming."

Emma's stomach rolled. "Right now, I'm blooming sick. But I guess you're right. I jumped into the ocean literally with both feet and I didn't let my natural caution hold me back. And now I'm sick as a dog."

"Well, no one said it would be perfect."

Emma's chuckle turned into a cough.

"I'll go and tell Andres. He's pacing the hallway and

there's not a lot of room out there. If it's any consolation, he's concerned. He seems like a decent guy."

Emma grabbed Tina's arm. "Wait. Tell me about your lawyer."

"He's good."

"How good?"

"Good enough that I won't be here tonight to hold your hand."

Emma let go. "You suck as a friend."

Tina got to her feet. "I do not. I'm letting your Latin friend hold your hand. Although I could swear I know him from somewhere."

"He's not going to want to hold my hand," Emma protested. No guy wanted to take care of a sickly woman. "If you tell him it will undermine everything I'm trying to do."

"On the way down here he offered to change rooms with me and when I told him that you were probably too sick to be interested in sex he assured me that his intentions were strictly platonic. I have to admit I'm impressed."

"And I'm anything but impressive. Whatever you do, don't let him come in here."

But of course Tina ignored Emma and let Andres come into the room where he solicitously took care of Emma and then held her throughout the night in her single bunk.

Even Emma was impressed.

7

EMMA WOKE UP from her catnap when Tina came storming into their cabin and slammed the door ferociously.

"Okay. I'm awake," Emma muttered.

"Sorry."

Emma stretched. "Why aren't you with Tyler?"

"Tyler? The man is a beast. I wouldn't spend another moment with him if he was the last man on this cruise ship. He's an arrogant jerk!"

"Your relationship's going that well?" Emma said dryly, getting to her feet.

"We don't have a relationship. I told you lawyers were trouble and I meant it. He got mad when I danced with Fabio. We were too close or something stupid. I couldn't believe it. We're not exclusive. I don't do exclusive for this very reason. Men get crazy and possessive." Tina waved her arms around to emphasize her point.

Emma yawned. "Get your lounge stuff and join me outside in the sun. We can commiserate together. Andres went off on a mysterious errand."

"I know. I saw him leave. Otherwise I would have knocked. I haven't seen you since you were throwing up the salt water. You okay?"

Emma wrapped her arms around herself. "Wonderful. I only wish the cruise was about two weeks longer. I can't believe I wasted a whole night being sick. And he wouldn't touch me this morning. Wanted me to recuperate. How could he be so dumb?"

"I can't wait to get off this ship." Tina rooted around in her suitcase, which was a jumble of bright colors. "His errand probably has to do with another woman since you were sick last night," Tina muttered.

"Hey! That's not fair."

"Sorry." Tina looked at Emma with true apology in her eyes. "I don't know how you manage to keep the faith when your dad dumps your mom and then Brad dumps you. Everyone we know has screwed-up or broken-up relationships."

Emma didn't answer.

"I want to have faith." Tina tossed one of her shoes down on the floor with a thud. "I do."

"Oh yeah, I got that."

"Why do you think I hang out with you? You're stronger than me. You keep getting kicked and you still believe. Me, I don't believe in anything. Except for you. I need your softer side to keep me from becoming a hardened bitch." The other shoe followed its mate to the floor with an even louder thud.

Emma took a deep breath. So much for her idea of confiding in Andres. Reality check. "You're not a bitch. And I was thinking of telling Andres my vital statistics and the fact that I'm a regular person."

"Good luck with that. Just try to convince him that the hot woman he's been with is really a plain Jane.

He'll laugh. Better to keep your doubts to yourself. This time you were the smart one, to keep it on a casual level. We should all leave this cruise with no addresses and no regrets."

"I guess Tyler screwed up."

"And I guess Andres is perfectly perfect," Tina growled.

Tina proceeded to fold a few of the pieces of clothing and stack them absently on the pillow, giving Emma a clue to just how much Tyler had upset her. Emma didn't even know Tina could fold clothes, she was such a devout fan of her dry cleaner.

A few minutes later they had a stack of clothes and Emma could contain her curiosity no longer. "If Tyler's so good, how could you let a little jealousy get between you? We've got two nights left."

Tina shrugged. "I never said he was good."

"Is he?"

"He gets the job done. He just doesn't understand my rules."

"You didn't hit him with the sperm-bank thing? It's gotta be a turn-off to be told you can be replaced by a test tube."

"Of course I didn't tell him."

"Well, that's good." Emma refolded a couple of shirts.

Tina got up and went to the minibar. She got out two miniature bottles of tequila. "Here, let's have a toast to the girlfriends who get us through the lonely nights." She came over to the bed and settled back down. "Cocks are definitely overrated."

"That's because you already had one today," Emma

said. They clinked the bottles together and sat companionably.

"Are you feeling okay?" Tina asked.

"I'm good." Emma put her bottle down. "I've come a long way and I owe it all to you." She reached over and hugged Tina, bottle and all.

"And you plan on going even further," Tina groused. "But you need to be careful. I recognize those stars in your eyes and you're going to get hurt badly if you assume Andres wants more than just a shipboard romance."

Emma put her hand up. "No, I'm sticking to my rules. We're not exchanging any of the sappy information people usually do. You know, the broken dreams and all of the soured relationships behind us." She didn't say how close she'd come to telling Andres everything and begging him to keep in touch. If Tina couldn't make the date thing work it couldn't be done. It would be better to make a clean break.

"That's the way to do it, girl. Don't let it run over into your regular life. Remember hiding in the break room after the fiasco with Brad?"

"I'm not likely to forget it." Emma picked up the palm-size bottle and took another swig of the tequila.

Tina patted Emma's knee. "I'm just worried about you. I don't know if you can take another disappointment so soon, and what would I do without my friend who believes? I'd get jaded."

"Honey, you are jaded." Emma softened her statement with a smile. "But where would a Shark be without her teeth? Now let's go out and sunbathe…like we're on a cruise in the Bahamas."

Without taking care to keep the freshly folded clothes in order, Tina began to dig through them. "I've got to find my turquoise suit. I know it's here somewhere. It's got this great belt that shows off my abs. You've got to show 'em while you've got 'em. After all, we won't always be young and beautiful enough to attract the men we want."

"What's the use of getting them if you can't keep them anyway?" But Emma handed Tina the top to the turquoise bikini. "I guess that anything other than living in the moment is a waste of time."

THE LAST NIGHT of the cruise was bittersweet. Emma and Andres danced and gambled and had a wonderful time, but Emma couldn't help but slip into a melancholy mood.

"Hey, *chula*. I've got one more surprise for you to-night."

Emma had lost track of the time, although it had to be long after midnight. She just didn't know how to say goodbye. "Okay."

"I made arrangements for us to enjoy one of the hot tubs."

"But they drain them in the evenings."

"It seems that you can get around the rules if Tina's dating the safety officer."

Emma smiled. Alone in the hot tub. Just one more adventure before they said goodbye. "That sounds wonderful."

They made their way up to the deck.

"It's hard to believe this deck is crawling with people during the day."

A shiver went through her that had nothing to do with the breeze and everything to do with anticipation.

She fidgeted. All she could think about was slipping naked into the hot tub with the stars all around her and his hands all over her.

"Emma?"

"Hum?"

"Am I losing you? Are you sleepy?"

"No." *Not a chance in hell.*

"What are you thinking about?"

"Trying out the hot tub." Being on top. *Wasn't that where The Shark would be?*

"Alone?" he teased.

She hesitated, not sure if she was brave enough to say what she was thinking. "Not exactly. I brought the glow-in-the-dark condoms."

"That sounds interesting. I hope you brought more than one." He let out his breath as if he'd been holding it for a while. "Because I'm going to take you as high as you've ever been."

She was afraid she'd go up in flames if he didn't stop talking. "You always make it sound like it's all for me. How come you're so generous?"

"A man gets his pleasure watching his woman enjoy herself. It's the biggest turn-on in the world. Your eyes will be like pools of midnight in your face. Your nipples will pucker and taste like honey in my mouth. I'll reach for you, and the soft sounds you'll make will be the only music I need to hear."

"This must be a vacation thing, right? You can't get this at home, that's for sure."

He laughed hoarsely. "Oh, *chula,* I want your curvy legs wrapped around me, the smooth curve of your ass in my hands, and to be deep, deep inside you. How can I not want someone as wonderful as you?"

She quivered. She'd probably have that orgasm he was talking about right here if he didn't shut up. "A man never wanted me this much."

He rubbed his hands together as if he didn't trust himself not to touch her. "*Querida*, that's most certainly true. I would fly across the country and sail the seas to be with you."

"That sounds awfully romantic, if a bit unlikely."

He looked down at her almost urgently. "What if I were telling you the truth? What if I'd come all this way for you? What if I knew you in another world? Would you dump me for my deceit when I couldn't help myself? Would you understand that I did it because I needed you so much, more than any other woman I've ever known?"

She didn't know what to say. It was as if they were having two different conversations. Maybe he was nervous about this, too. Then she heard the footsteps she'd been unconsciously listening for. An Italian man came up to them and spoke quietly. "It's the tub by the minibar on the back of the ship. It's the most secluded. You've got thirty minutes. It's all I can do. My shift is over soon."

He walked away without another word.

Emma watched him go. "Do you think we'll get caught? I don't want to get him in trouble."

"He obviously thinks we can get away with it. I have

a feeling we're not the only ones who wanted some privacy on deck for a price.

"Are you still up for this?" He held out his hand.

She rose unsteadily. "Should we get some towels?"

He practically bolted over to one of the towel racks, which had already been refilled. She grinned. His boyish ways were wonderfully disarming when his masculinity got too intense. He'd brought her both pleasure and laughter, a beautiful and heady combination.

On shaking legs, Emma followed Andres towards the back of the ship and the hot tub.

A few minutes later they stood beside the tub, looking at the dark landscape of the ship and the stars above them. She wondered if she had the guts to just strip down to her skin right here in front of him.

He must have read her indecision in her body language. "Emma, we don't have to do this. We can go back to my stateroom. I don't want you to worry about anything."

That gave her all of the courage she needed. She pulled the skinny black dress over her head.

He turned and looked at her bare skin, his eyes widening at the sight of the skimpy pink thong she had on. Her nipples stood at attention in the breeze.

Staring as if he'd never seen a naked woman before, Andres just stood there.

It made Emma feel brave and she kept eye contact with him as she reached down and pushed the thong over her hips. She didn't even look down as the thong fell to the deck. Naked, illuminated only by the night sky, she stood proudly before him.

His eyes were too dark to read, but he seemed almost shy, clutching the towels to his chest like a shield.

His vulnerability gave her the courage to reach out and run her hand over the front of his shorts. "We only have a little time out here."

He dropped the towels. His clothes followed the path of the towels onto the deck.

Naked, he reached out as if to grab her up in his arms. She almost panicked. "You might…drop me," she told him, taking an instinctive step away from him. She wanted him fiercely, but now the bold woman wavered.

He did grab her, easily because she'd literally backed herself into the hot tub, lifting her effortlessly. He walked up the stairs with her cradled in his arms like a child.

She felt anything but safe. Yet all of her fears fled.

He put her down in the water, standing in the sea-water up to his thighs while he made sure she was comfortable. The difference in the temperature of the water and the air caused her to slide more deeply into the warmth. None of the lights in the hot tub were on, and Emma was daring, wanton, hungry…

"Is it warm enough?" She raised one leg out of the water to rest her foot on the side of the tub leaving her parted legs open to the sexual sensation of the swirling water.

His eyes were apparently adjusted to the starlight because he ran his hand unerringly along the length of that long sensitive leg.

"I'm burning up."

With her eyes she followed the path of that dark arrow of hair, to his erect penis.

She raised her face so she could meet his eyes. The fact that she couldn't see his expression made it all the more mysterious.

Holding on to the sides of the tub, she stretched her arms up, hoping he was focusing on the way her breasts bobbed nearly on the top of the water. "I want to feel you."

In a fluid motion he submerged in the tub, coming up between her legs. He sat right there, giving her a chance to entwine her smooth legs with his hairy ones, the textural difference seeming greater in the water, which intrigued her immensely. She ran her hand over his leg, knee to thigh and then explored the length of his arousal. He shifted under her attention, making her feel wonderfully powerful.

"Will you sit on my lap, *querida?*"

"I would love to." To her surprise she was absolutely ready to do exactly that.

He reached out and laid a hand on her shoulder. Emma quivered, longing for him to run his hand down over her breast.

She lifted her leg and put it over his thigh. He urged her to him and the buoyant water brought her around to settle firmly in his lap.

She didn't think. She kissed him. He tasted smooth and silky, but underneath there was a thread of intense heat. He became a craving, a dangerous one. Boldly she stroked with her tongue, unable to get enough of his taste.

His hands stayed on her shoulders as she pressed closer to ease the ache in her nipples. He groaned and touched her, thumbing her nipples, which were tight and tingling.

Where the effervescent bubbles of the hot tub had

primed her flesh, the firmness of his touch was sheer heaven. Her nipples throbbed. He kissed her mouth, the side of her neck and then he lowered his head into the water to suckle her nipples. His mouth felt warmer than the tub water. His teeth teased her.

"Here, I want you to feel this." He pushed her around on the seat until she faced the side of the tub, her knees hitting the marble side. "What?" she asked, suddenly feeling vulnerable.

"Right here."

"I don't know…" She trailed off as he came up behind her, pushing against her with both hands, which held her bottom. His penis nestled firmly against her cheeks. She shifted and he made a noise in his throat as if it hurt him to be so close to her. As if he wanted her desperately.

His hands came up to plunder her breasts. She gasped. Her nipples tingled. She felt weightless, boneless. Her head fell back against his shoulder.

It was then that she became aware of the jet situated directly between her legs. There wasn't much water pressure since her knees at the wall kept her about six inches from the explosion of water, but those insidious bubbles, they bounced one at a time, in urgent succession, off her aroused feminine flesh.

That small ache built and built… She writhed, trying to get away from the swelling, which threatened to overwhelm her.

And then she let the sensation take her away…

It took her a minute of lolling against the side of the tub in his arms to acclimate.

"Emma? *Chula*?"

"I'm glad you were here to hold me up because I probably would have happily drowned."

He squeezed her bottom. kneading the globes. The jet wasn't positioned in exactly the same place but she could feel the sensation, her flesh waking up for another round. He pushed her higher.

"Oh, don't do that."

"Ah, but you liked it so much."

"Yes, but I want to put one of those condoms on you and then I want to…"

"What?"

"I want to be on top."

He squeezed her tightly. "We'll get to the condoms. I just want to do that again. I loved the soft sounds you made when you came apart in my arms."

"I did *not* make sounds. I'm trying to be quiet since we're breaking the rules and could end up in the brig." But those same sounds escaped her as she wriggled and writhed against the sensations building inside her. The jet was closer and hitting exactly the right spot. "Andres…" she protested.

"I've got you, baby."

Because she was with Andres, she just let it happen. The jets massaged and she wriggled, she panted, she moaned. And just when she thought she'd scream he turned her around, pressing her against him.

She grabbed him, almost panting, starving for him. She had both hands on his silky erection, stroking him up and down. He was so ready. And she wanted to see him dressed in nothing but one of those outrageous condoms. "Andres?"

"What?" He sounded like he was in pain. The pain of holding back if the size of his erection was any indication of his desire.

"Where are the condoms?" she asked urgently.

He handed her a small package, which she opened quickly. Andres stood up out of the water and then she reached for his silky flesh. The condom went on smoothly, Emma almost shuddering with desire as she rolled it on.

"Does it seem silly?" The glow-in-the-dark condom looked kind of like a light sword, a large vigorous saber in the dark. She stroked it ardently.

"Not when it pleases you so. Do you think I care which condom we use? I'm just thrilled that you thought of making love to me in the hot tub," he said hoarsely, as he sat down, pushing her firmly, deeply into the water right on top of the jets at the bottom of the tub.

Her head was just above the water level and he suckled her lips, the water rolling between them. Desire flooded her senses as down below her the flood of tiny bubbles teased and taunted her already sensitized flesh.

When she looked down all she could see was his penis glowing beneath the water like a beacon. His desire was so evident it made her quiver with need. "I can see how much you want me," she moaned. "And I want you, too, so much. All of you."

He placed kisses along her jaw, driving her crazy. She wrapped her arm around his shoulders and rubbed her aching nipples against the crisp hair on his chest. He stroked the heat between her legs.

She half moaned, half laughed. "This is so perfect," she panted. "You make all of my fantasies come true."

"Baby, you're a dream come true."

The pressure built inside her, distracting her from the fact he hadn't call her any of those Spanish endearments. Instead she tried to squirm away from his touch. "Don't, I can barely stand it and I don't know if I can be quiet this time."

"Don't worry, sweetheart. There's no one here but us."

Emma angled the burning center of herself against the cock she so craved until he was fully, firmly inside her. She wriggled around some more until his penis filled her to the hilt. Rocking against him, she almost cried out with the joy of being a part of him.

He put his hands on her hips and set the rhythm, up and down, the bubbles cascaded around them, teasing her flesh.

Hot, wet and hard, Andres fulfilled all of Emma's fantasies. With his last thrust, his fire consumed her, and she boiled over in a gush of pleasure.

Emma and Tina were packing, their entire colorful island wardrobe spread out on their bunks.

"So when are you saying goodbye to Andres?" Tina asked, carelessly shoving the clothes Emma had folded for her into her designer bags.

"We already did." Emma felt listless and she just couldn't find the energy to pack the way she usually did. She watched Tina with envy. Why couldn't she just shove her stupid stuff in the suitcase like Tina did? What would it hurt?

"Was it quick and painless that way?"

"It was my idea. I didn't want to drag it out. I didn't

even give him my e-mail or anything, and he didn't offer his." Emma sniffed. "It was just a fling. Not romance. Besides, I think he was lying to me."

"Why do you say that?"

"Because last night in the hot tub his Spanish sort of broke down and he started calling me sweetheart and baby. And I swear I've heard his voice somewhere before."

"You did the right thing." Tina walked into the bathroom to get one of her makeup bags. "Men don't believe in the L-word. They have only one agenda, the agenda between the sheets. Women can either adopt the same agenda, or they can be resentful when they discover it's true."

Emma sank down on her bed. "I'm just trying to protect the fantasy. If I were to ask him about himself and he told me that he's some car salesman who got his tan from a tanning bed and his Spanish from a college course it would spoil all of my perfect memories."

"He *was* damn good." Tina zipped around the small stateroom, full of nervous energy.

Emma wondered why Tina was all hyped up. Maybe saying goodbye to Tyler hadn't been so painless. Perhaps the cruise would be a difficult memory for both of them. "It was too good to be true. Once Andres got to know the real me, he'd be disappointed. He thinks I'm a wild, crazy, sexy woman who has sex in public, wears thong bikinis and knows how to keep a guy interested, when I'm not really that person at all."

This time a tear slipped out and Emma used a tropical print top she'd bought in Nassau while shopping with

Andres to dry her eyes, which only made her want to cry harder.

"But you *are* the sexy woman he knows. Everything you did was honestly you. It's just a side of you that you hadn't explored before." Tina hovered.

Emma sniffed. "I guess so."

"You should definitely stop crying now." Tina seemed almost frantic.

"Relax. I'm not going to start sobbing and beating my breast in front of you."

Emma scooped up the remainder of her unfolded clothing and dumped it in her suitcase. "I'm going to be okay."

"No, you're not okay. I've never seen you so upset. You're actually putting unfolded clothes in your suitcase and that's after you already folded all of my stuff for about the tenth time. If you need to see Andres again then go and tell him, get his e-mail address. What's the worst thing that can happen?"

"He might find out that I'm a phony."

Tina put her hand on Emma's shoulder. "You're the most genuine person I know, and if a change of clothes or actually enjoying yourself during sex means a girl's a phony then all the women on the cruise were guilty. Think about it. Is there anything you've done on this cruise you wouldn't be willing to repeat at home with the right guy?"

Emma shook her head. She'd love to repeat all of it. Especially the part where she'd been on top. She really had come a long way on this cruise. In fact she'd done almost everything she set out to do. So why did she feel so let down?

"Then do one more brave and daring thing—go to his stateroom and exchange personal information. How scary can that be?"

Emma thought about everything else she'd done. A slow smile spread across her face. "Not so bad."

"Then go get him, girl."

"Okay." Emma looked around. Did she need anything?

Tina grabbed her. "Wait. Just pull this top down lower. No sense in letting a cleavage opportunity go to waste."

Emma rushed out and headed for the elevators. She dodged people and luggage in the crowded halls. Finally, she arrived a few doors down from his stateroom. She slowed, took a few deep breaths, ran her fingers through her swinging hair and...

The door was open. The room was totally cleared out.

Emma stepped inside, closed the door and went over to the bed they'd shared. He'd pulled the coverlet up. Absently she smoothed it.

He was gone. Forever.

She had no way to get in touch with him. Because of her fears. Tina was right. Emma had finally become the woman she'd always dreamed of being right up until the end and then she'd let herself down.

"I can't believe I let you go," she told the empty room in a broken voice. Sinking down on the bed, she buried her face in his pillow. His scent filled her head. She curled up in the fetal position.

And cried.

Until Tina came and hauled her away.

8

BRIGHT AND EARLY Monday morning Emma dragged herself into the office feeling as if she had the hangover of the century. But it wasn't the amount of alcohol she'd consumed on the cruise which had her feeling down, it was the stupidity of leaving Andres without any way to contact him.

Well, it had seemed like the bold, confident thing to do at the time.

She pushed her overflowing in-box over to the far corner of the desk and got up to see if Tina was having a similar case of vacation letdown.

She stopped in the break room which was full of coffee drinkers. Reaching up she felt the smooth swing of her straight hair. She wore her usual uniform of a skirt and blouse, but the blouse was from the islands, and she'd ditched the panty hose. Strappy heels complimented her lightly tanned skin.

"Hi Emma. You're looking good." She turned to see Lance Levine. Lance the letch, the assistants had dubbed him. He should have been considered a prime ass, but he was a very attractive man, and rich, so some of the women put up with him, despite his wandering hands.

She gave him a smile. "Thank you." Word was that he was very sexually experienced. But then she was no slouch in the sexual department herself since she'd added beaches, bondage and hot tubs to her repertoire.

"Heard you had a Spanish hunk following you around," one of the young assistants gushed at her as she put on earphones playing loud, pulsing music. "I guess you're over Brad the jerk."

Emma just nodded at the girl.

The girl adjusted her earphones. "Way to rock, baby."

Emma made her way to the refrigerator and grabbed a bottle of cold water, greeting a few other coworkers on her way out the door and down the hall.

Feeling like a different woman, confident, exciting and the author of all possibilities, Emma strutted down the hallway. The cruise might have been about fantasy, so everything felt extraordinary there, but some of the cruise had spilled over into her regular world. The experiment seemed to be working—all the evidence pointed to a bolder, more confident Emma.

She smiled.

Then she felt it. That pang in her chest. She rubbed the spot over her heart. It still ached for Andres. Could she do it again? Be that sensual, confident partner to another. What was wrong with turning the volume all the way up? Andres thought she could.

Unfortunately he was long gone.

Outside Tina's office she heard a familiar voice and looked around. Andres was haunting her of course. Why wouldn't he? He was the most passionate, most intense lover she'd ever had. How could she expect to ever forget him?

Squaring her shoulders she waltzed through Tina's office door, which was ajar. "Tina, you know we never got around to getting that henna tattoo in Key West. And I definitely earned it."

She stopped dead. Andres was here, at *her* law firm, standing by Tina's desk as though he belonged here.

He was actually here.

The breath seemed to be sucked out of her body like the surf getting pulled back into the ocean. For a moment she even saw the stars over the beach.

Get a grip.

"Emma!" Tina sounded distressed.

Emma stepped into the room and grabbed the back of a chair for support. Tina and Andres were frozen at the desk like people stuck on pause.

"Emma, I'm sorry." His voice flowed over her like the rumble of the surf and all of the details slid into place.

Emma tapped her finger against her chin. She knew that voice. No wonder he'd instantly grabbed her attention. She'd been drooling over the sound of that voice over the phone for weeks. The voice of the Acc-U-Tech guy. The guy who'd developed the program they were buying for the firm.

Heat flooded her face. She'd often thought he should be doing phone sex not spout technobabble. And she'd fantasized about him endlessly—of course the reality was so much better. He looked great with those dress slacks hugging his tight ass.

She stepped all the way into the room and slammed

the door behind her. She smiled, her face tight and stiff. "How's it going, Andres? It's quite a surprise to see you here."

"I can explain."

Did his face have a greenish tinge or was it the fluorescent lights? "Or should I call you Tony?"

"Emma, please listen to me."

"I don't need you to explain anything. I know who you are. You're Tony Enderlin from Acc-U-Tech. And you developed the new program. But you weren't scheduled to install it…" The last of it came out almost a stutter.

Emma bit her lip. She felt so exposed.

Exactly the way she'd felt when they'd caught Brad in the work room with the bimbo clerk. As though she'd been the one caught in nothing but a skirt on top of the copy machine after hours.

Tony didn't look as if he felt much better than she did but she'd be damned if she'd feel sorry for him.

"I would have told you." He put his hands out as if in supplication. "I did tell you before we got into the hot tub."

She waved her arms in the air. "So, you spilled some romantic babble about flying the world and sailing the seas. You knew it wouldn't mean anything specific to me."

"I *told* you. You just didn't want to know me or anything real about me. You only wanted a fantasy, a mysterious stranger who couldn't give you any more than short-term…" He looked over at Tina.

"Sex?" Emma said pointedly, smoothing down her hair; it seemed to be standing on end. "I can't believe this," she muttered. "I can't believe I've been this stupid again! All I wanted was to be more sophisticated and sexy, and I'm a schmuck all over again! All men lie. None of you can be trusted." The tide of anger rose to engulf her.

"You might want to keep your voice down or you'll be hiding out in the break room indefinitely." Tina looked from one of them to the other and then slowly got up out of her chair. "And I'll just leave you two alone. You have a lot to discuss."

She glared at Tony.

Tina turned to her and explained, "I told him this morning when I realized where I'd seen him before that you wouldn't understand. I warned him he was better off going back to Acc-U-Tech. And I was telling him just now that you'd fillet him and that I'd help you."

With one last hard look at Tony, Tina opened the door and stalked out. The slamming of the door was followed by the sharp sound of her heels on the tile outside.

Emma and Tony stared at each other over the back of the chair until the sound faded.

"I *should* fillet you," Emma finally spat at him. "You shouldn't be here. Not at my company. Not in my space." She managed to say it confidently but her legs were shaking.

"That's how you wanted it. You wanted a stranger. I just went along with you." He looked haggard, as if he hadn't slept since the cruise. "You don't know how I've felt knowing I might lose you all over again once you knew the truth."

"You never had me to lose. You agreed, it was just going to be sex and you would walk away!" How could she be so angry that he hadn't really walked out of her life when just moments ago she'd been cursing herself for letting him do just that? How could she want to throw herself into his arms and strangle him at the same time? Where had the logical Emma gone? And who was the stranger in her shoes who wanted to walk all over Andres/Tony in spike heels until he bled? The way she felt that she was bleeding.

"I knew I'd see you again. And I hinted about it over and over again."

"Yet you agreed!" Her voice rose at the thought of how much it had hurt when he'd casually agreed not to exchange personal information, in essence, agreed never to talk to her or touch her again.

"I wanted you to have your fantasy."

She smiled grimly. "Of course, you were all about lies and fantasy."

His smile was half-hearted. "I would have been anything you asked me to be for just a moment in your arms."

"More fiction? Really, you don't have to bother!" Her voice actually got shrill, so she sucked in a breath like an asthmatic. "It was just sex and I'm so glad I never had any actual expectations. Men are scum. They have only one goal—to get a woman into bed," she snarled.

"You must know that it's not true. I wanted to be with you in so many ways."

She straightened to her full height. She couldn't believe him. It didn't make any sense to believe him. "You're just like Brad."

"Brad? You think I'm like that scumbag who cheated on you?"

"How do know what he did to me?"

"I was here in the office for a few days before the cruise, spinning my wheels waiting for Melissa to decide it was time to install the program. I got an earful from every lawyer in the place while I defragged their computers. It was the gossip of the month."

Tears burned the back of her throat. Her eyes watered but she didn't cry, wouldn't cry. Tony knew all about her humiliation here at the office. "I didn't want you to know about that. I don't want you to feel sorry for me."

"I didn't." He sounded angry, almost bitter. "And I don't, because the amazing woman I met on the cruise doesn't need any sympathy or pity."

She tapped her fingers against her chin again, listening, really listening, for the first time since her temper had blazed to life. Another first. She'd never had such a passionately angry response in her life. "You're right."

"Yeah, I am, and I won't let you reduce our relationship to something impersonal. I never felt more apprehensive in my life than when I left that boat without telling you everything. But there just didn't seem to be a good time. We just sort of rushed along on a vacation high. It was incredible. Amazing."

Anguish grabbed her by the guts. It *had* been amazing, but she couldn't afford to admit it. "We never really knew each other." She thought she might need an entire roll of Tums.

"I thought we got to know each other rather intimately." He crossed his arms over his chest. His dark eyes blazed some unspoken emotion.

She wrapped her arms around her waist. "Not really. I didn't know who you were."

"Emma. You wanted it that way."

She looked up again, mesmerized by that voice.

"But I know you. I know your eyes go all hazy when you get aroused and I know the way you liked to be stroked along your beautiful back. You're ticklish behind your knees and you sigh in your sleep."

She forced herself to smile, despite the fact that it felt like a feral grin. Caving in on this bullshit was out of the question. Neither her weak knees nor the pain in her gut, were going to convince her that he was any more trustworthy than Brad, any more worthy of a relationship, or any more capable of happily ever after than her father had been, though she yearned for those things.

Why couldn't she learn her lesson? Internalize her humiliation and use it as a shield? Be like Tina? She absolutely needed to be on guard against giving into the whole romantic fantasy.

"None of this emotional stuff is important. I had no expectations. We had sex and now it's over. Great sex," she felt compelled to add. "But you'll go home to Colorado, tomorrow or the day after, so it really doesn't change anything. It's still goodbye and good luck."

Tony actually looked hurt.

Why should I care?

He spoke up in a quiet voice. "I came to install the program myself because of how much I enjoyed talking to you on the phone. But you were hiding out because of your humiliation over Brad. I couldn't even get close to you. Then the ticket and the cruise just sort of fell in my lap."

"My humiliation? Maybe I was just using him for sex."

"The way you used me?"

Emma stiffened at the blow. How could he think she was capable of using him? So she adopted Tina's attitude. "I thought it was mutual. We used each other and had a wonderfully romantic cruise. What's the problem?"

He stared at her for a moment, then hitched his hand in his belt. "No problem. And no reason why we couldn't take up where we left off. I could touch you again. Run my hands and mouth over your breasts. Lift your skirt. Slide the thong down between your legs."

Her mouth fell open to the point that she sputtered, "I don't think so." She backed into the door behind her.

But the heat was there between her legs. Her traitorous body missed his touch, his preoccupation with every part of her, and most of all his deep, slow penetration. Her breasts swelled above their underwire.

"Why not, *chula*?" Those dark eyes challenged her.

She tugged on her neckline, wishing the summer material was heavy enough to hide her body's response. "Apparently I was right-on. I didn't think it would be the same once we got off the cruise, Andres. Where did you get the absurd name, anyway? And were you just practicing your high-school Spanish or what?"

"It's my middle name. My grandmother's Hispanic. She babysat me when I was young and spoke Spanish to me. She always called me by my middle name."

"Convenient."

"Nothing about you turns out to be convenient. You're as complicated as hell." He gazed into her face.

"What are you saying?" Emma tugged on her hair.

He leaned in next to her and whispered, "What if I promise to make it very pleasurable for you while I'm needing you? Will you please give me a chance to explain?"

"I don't think so. I can't afford to cause any more gossip here at the office."

He pulled away. "I'm sorry you feel that way. I guess we'll just keep our professional distance as we work together on the installation of the new program."

"I don't think it's necessary for us to work closely together. Our in-house tech guy is more than qualified to assist you. Besides, you're just milking the company if you're going from computer to computer. Everyone knows that's not necessary within a network."

He looked almost embarrassed. "This is a very important field test and I'm not charging your boss for the extra time. She gets all of the individual computers purged. I get the program running at optimal capacity and I get a chance to see what kind of real-world problems my on-site techs are going to have."

"Melissa went for that explanation?"

"I couldn't very well admit that I came all this way just to meet her assistant." He crowded her slowly.

"We can't work together." There was nowhere to go.

"I'm not going to accept the tech. I want you." He didn't touch her, but his eyes promised her things she shouldn't think about. "Do you know how much porn I found on these lawyers' computers? All sorts of things that a sexually mature woman might want to experiment with if she had a willing partner."

Emma shivered. They'd done some exciting things in the name of fantasy, things she still dreamed about.

There was one last excuse. "I can't date another guy at work. I've already learned that lesson. You don't need me. I'll talk to Melissa."

He looked at her with serious eyes. "You do that, but I intend to do everything in my power to keep you by my side and change your mind about our…connection. I'll convince Melissa that you're indispensable. That I need you desperately." His eyes flicked over her body.

Had he touched her? She felt as if he had. She had to squelch her naiveté. There was no such thing as a connection or the right guy. If she was lucky she'd have a couple of pretty children before her first divorce. If she was smart she'd remember Tina's misery on the ship. There were no happy endings out there. Not for an ordinary girl, not even for an extraordinary girl.

EMMA SPENT the rest of her day in a haze. The last few hours were spent pushing papers around on her desk trying not to think of Tony messing with a computer just a few feet down the hall.

"Emma, I need you to come into my office for a minute." Melissa stuck her head through Emma's door, taupe silk suit buttoned up to her chin, pink pearls the size of nickels around her neck, designer pen in hand and wearing a grimace.

Sighing, Emma obediently gathered up the calendar and her notepad to make a record of what her boss wanted. Melissa rarely loosened up; in fact she looked like an old-fashioned principal in designer suits. Absolutely no one at the firm underestimated her intelligence or her priorities.

Inside the inner office, Emma carefully closed the door behind her. Melissa tapped her pen on the desk, a nervous habit that boded ill for whoever or whatever had aggravated her.

Emma had been expecting this ever since Tony had taken Melissa to lunch. Surely her boss needed her too much to just hand her over to him? Didn't she?

"Emma?" Melissa looked up over one of her many pairs of granny glasses that coordinated with every suit she owned. Today's choice were gold-plated and slipping down her elegant nose.

Emma straightened up and patted the daily planners on her lap. "What calendar do we need? The court schedule or the office schedule? I'm a little behind because of my vacation so I'll have to work harder to catch up."

"You know how important the new program is to the firm?" More tapping.

Emma nodded.

"I've heard that you refused to help Mr. Enderlin install it and make sure it's running smoothly. I believe this is just a rumor because we both know what a professional you are. So where do you think such a silly rumor got started?" The tapping became more energetic.

"I have no idea. But there's no way in hell I'll help Mr. Enderlin finish the project." Emma put her hand over her mouth. Where had that come from? Was this more fallout from the cruise? Because this was not the best time or place to have developed a backbone.

Melissa dropped the pen and for a moment, her mouth hung open in a very unprofessional, very un-principal-like way. "What did you say?" Melissa said a second later when she recovered her usual composure.

"He deceived me. I can't work with him. He's another Brad." Somehow it came out sounding so logical. Emma blinked. She actually sounded kind of lawyerlike.

Melissa slowly picked up her pen. Emma felt the laser gaze that usually made her feel as though she was back in the third grade.

"So the rumors about the cruise are accurate?"

Not for the first time Emma resented the lawyer habit of turning everything into a question. She crossed her arms over her chest. "It depends on what rumors you're talking about. I met Andres, I mean Tony Enderlin, on the cruise but nothing happened."

"Then why can't you work with him?"

"I mean that nothing sexual happened." Emma hoped her face wasn't red, but her skin felt as if it was on fire. "I didn't know he was the computer guy. I couldn't have known. How could I have known?"

"What you do on your vacation is none of my business. But what you do in this office reflects on me. I'm aware of your ambition to become a paralegal and I think it's a good plan. Once you're finally ready, I might even be able to help by providing more flexible work hours and maybe even some help with the educa-tional expenses in exchange for your coming back to work at this firm. I would only do this because I'm impressed with your performance as my assistant and because I believe you're an asset to this firm." The pen tapped a slow, steady warning for Emma not to blow the opportunity Melissa offered.

Emma resisted the urge to shift from foot to foot. "That's very generous."

"But—" Melissa leaned forward, glasses perched on the end of her nose "—Mr. Enderlin's boss says he's brilliant. We're lucky to have him here. He's the best and I like the idea of getting their best man."

Emma could just imagine what Tina would say when she told her how she'd blown an opportunity for the firm to help her become a paralegal because she couldn't face Tony, in the office. If Tina didn't kill her, Emma would probably have to slit her own wrists because she'd promised herself she'd take opportunities to advance herself.

And now everything was backfiring because it seemed that Tony was tied up with all of her goals. How could this have happened?

"Emma?"

"There's no problem. I'm looking forward to working with Mr. Enderlin. When we spoke on the phone I found him friendly and knowledgeable. I'm sure we'll fit, I mean work, very well together." Emma almost choked when she remembered how well they'd fitted together. And how much pleasure they'd shared.

"Great. That's all I wished to speak to you about." The pen was no longer tapping. Instead, Melissa ran her fingers over the smooth surface of the pen.

Emma knew this was a sign of Melissa having resolved the problem and drew a sigh of relief as she practically slunk out of her boss's office.

When she got to her desk she dropped her head in her hands and groaned.

9

"I CAN'T BELIEVE how cold you are." Tony moved the mouse to the appropriate icon on the computer screen. "Nothing like my Emma, the one I met on the beach."

"I don't want to talk about it." Emma tried to find a more comfortable position in the high-backed chair in front of the huge oak desk. But he hovered above her making her nervous.

"Come on. You're not exactly being fair."

Emma resisted the urge to bash him over the head with the metal paperweight of a golfer on Morrison's desk. The lawyer came from money and spent more time on the course than in court. Yet he had a desk the size of a bed.

"If we're going to install this program effectively, then we should behave professionally. We should pretend we have no history. You promised me that you wouldn't refer to anything that happened on the cruise." It was the only thing that could get her through the week.

He grinned. "'If we're going to be professional'—you've been hiding behind that phrase and I'm tired of it. No way am I going to be professional. I'm going to seduce you."

She shook her head until her hair swung. "No you're not. We're just installing this program and then you're leaving to go home to Colorado." Her voice rose.

"I'm not leaving yet. I still have a lot to do."

"You're procrastinating, playing with all of these individual PCs. Just install the damn thing and go home."

"You'd love for me to do that. It would confirm that I'm the kind of guy you think would pick you up on a singles' cruise, but I'm not a player. And I'm not leaving. Not yet. Not until you remember how it feels when I tie you up and you are so wet and sweet. I'm going to tell you every time we're alone how much I want to unbutton that pretty white blouse and fill my hands with your breasts. I want to suckle you through the material and then see the way it clings to you. Then I want to—"

Emma got up, unapologetically pushing him out of her way. She looked out in the hallway to see if any lawyers were lurking.

She'd been leaving the door open. But if anyone had overheard his comments she'd once again be the laughingstock of the office.

Once she'd established that there was no one outside the door, she leaned against the doorjamb, considering the situation.

Impossible. This situation was impossible.

She tried to drape her arm across her chest to hide the way her nipples had hardened. "This is not going to work. I think I'd rather lose my job than put up with this harassment."

"Harassment?" He looked very concerned. "That's a

pretty serious accusation. Are you planning on siccing Tina on me? Taking me to court?"

"No. But I don't want to remember the things we did on the cruise. Please don't bring it up again."

"Why? Because you miss me? The way I make you feel? The way we were together?"

"I never said that."

"You don't have to. I miss you, too."

She felt a bit panicky. "Don't. I meant to leave the romance and the mystery of the cruise behind me. It's better that way."

"Why?"

Why? She floundered for a minute. "Because I don't want to get…attached. Looking for a relationship is what got me in trouble in the first place. And I'm not going to repeat my mistakes at work." Who was she trying to convince, Tony or herself?

She'd gotten stuck with him to keep Melissa happy and to keep the bargain she'd made with herself to forward her career. But what was she going to do with these feelings he still roused in her every chance they were alone?

"I know you still want me."

She did want him, desperately. Every word just conjured up another need. And he could please her anywhere, anytime, with any sort of toy. She felt as if she were sliding down a very slippery slope and grasping at straws. "I—I can't afford another unpleasant association like Brad. I value my job too much to put it in jeopardy and now they want to help me go to school."

"I'm not technically an employee. And I'm outta here in a couple of weeks."

A couple of weeks? Hadn't he said a week? "I can't wait that long." She needed him gone.

"Neither can I. I want you so badly."

She curled her fingers into her palms. Of course he'd misunderstood. Well, two could play that game. "Maybe I'm just missing sex in general, not you specifically."

"I think you're lying through those pretty teeth. I think you're afraid of having sex with me. I don't think you do casual sex. I think you're just talking yourself into it."

She straightened. "I do, too!" But she wasn't so sure. Lance the letch had petted her butt when she'd gone in to get her water from the employee fridge and she'd backed away from him. He didn't make her feel the way Tony did.

Everything seemed to be wrapped around Tony. And that was damned dangerous.

"Then we'll just have to practice having casual sex."

She sucked in her breath. "We already did."

"That was on the cruise, a fantasy. You'll have to prove it all over again in real life."

She shook her head. How in the world had she boxed herself into this corner?

His look challenged her. "Meet me tonight after the office closes."

"Why? What will it prove? That I didn't learn anything from the Brad fiasco?"

"Meet me outside the janitor's closet at seven o'clock after work, and trust that I'm not as dumb as Brad."

"This is not a good idea. I won't do this."

"Don't worry, *chula.* We'll keep the rules the same

as on the cruise. We'll just pleasure each other until we're sated without any sort of commitment. We won't even date."

"Thanks," she said with irony. "I guess it's a good offer but I'm not going anywhere near the janitor's closet."

SHE HADN'T MEANT to stay late but her in-box had been full and it had taken her a while to clear things up. That was the reason that she was walking out of the building at seven, by way of the janitor's closet.

"You look so beautiful today. I couldn't take my eyes off your incredible legs long enough to do my job."

Emma stopped to take in the sight of Tony leaning against the door to the janitor's office as if he were the romantic lead in a movie.

"I didn't wear this skirt for your benefit. I always dress professionally for the office."

"I even love the crisp white blouse. It's been making me crazy because I can almost see through it."

"I don't want to do this."

"Yes you do." To Emma's surprise Tony took out a key and opened the door to the janitor's closet. "Because you're a sensual woman with a taste for experimentation."

"In a janitor's closet?"

"Hey it'll be harder on me than you since I'm claustrophobic."

"You are not."

"Yes I am, and if you put your hand over my heart you'll feel how hard it's beating, *querida*."

The Spanish love word made her knees go weak. At

least she thought it was a love word. "What does *querida* mean?"

"It means, my lover."

"I'm not your lover."

"You were when I was using that word. I touched you with all of the hunger of a lover, all of the need. I know you remember."

She remembered. Man, she had to get a grip on something. How could she have developed such strong sexual needs in such a short time? And hadn't Tony fulfilled all of her desires thus far? Couldn't she just make sure she wouldn't revert to the old, inhibited Emma? Just this once? Surely no one would ever know.

Tony glanced down each of the hallways to make sure they were still alone, protecting his woman, though he wanted her so fiercely he could barely think coherently. Every since he'd left the cruise he'd been worried that he'd never get to touch her again, and he needed to. Badly.

He opened the door and then took several steps inside. She came in close behind him and he heard her hit the mop bucket with her foot before he got the lights on. He grabbed her, just barely keeping her upright. "Be careful. You don't want to break a leg in here."

"No, that wouldn't be discreet."

She felt like heaven in his arms and he knew he wouldn't be able to sell the casual sex thing to himself, no matter what he told her. Nothing about this relationship was casual. But Emma was determined to be a hard sell and he didn't even know what he had to offer. They lived in different parts of the country and they both liked their lives and their jobs. And great sex did not make a relationship. He needed more from her; he just didn't know how to define what he wanted.

"Hey, I should trade with Max the janitor. I'd have a bigger office."

Tony didn't answer. He couldn't think about the size of the place. He steered her against the wall so he could pass and he closed the door gently, while pushing in the locking mechanism. He was determined to ignore the way his hands shook.

So he concentrated on her—the way she cocked her head to look up at the portable shelves covered with cleaning supplies, the way her clothing clung to her slim figure, the length of her legs under that modest skirt. He hoped she was wearing another thong, just a scrap of damp silk.

He'd make sure it was damp.

"I could use some shelves like these. I wonder where Max got them."

Tony flipped off the light. Then he sucked in his breath when she brushed up against him. He hoped it was desire and not the claustrophobia.

"We could have another fantasy. We could be anywhere you would like to go." *Anywhere but here*, he thought, feeling the dark walls closing in.

But then she leaned into him, her body warm and pliable against his, and the pulse started pounding in his throat. This time he knew it was due to her.

"Andres? Your heart is pounding. Is it because we're in a closet?"

"We're not just in a closet. We're hiding out during a big fancy party because we want each other so much we can't wait. But we can't afford to be discovered. Everyone will talk. I'm going to push you up against the wall and have my way with you, and then after you've come in a shuddering climax in my arms, we'll go back outside and pretend that nothing has happened."

He heard her take a shaky breath. "Why do you want me so much?"

Was there a quiver in her voice?

"I wish I knew. I just have to have you."

And he did have her. Right here. His hands came around her waist in a protective manner.

Emma didn't know why she'd never noticed how large his hands were—they easily spanned her waist. She shivered, suddenly back on the deck of the ship, bathed in moonlight.

Or maybe at his glittering party with music and people just beyond the door and only the two of them inside.

Desire swept through her as Tony ran his fingers up the back of her neck and into her hair. She tingled, enjoying each caress. She could feel all her control slipping away. "Tony, turn on the light," she protested, abruptly afraid of her heated response.

"If you don't like the party then think of our moonlit beach. We can go back there." He kissed her neck. "Only this time we can go as far as we want."

"We can't ever go back."

His hands moved over the light material of her blouse, running down her side. Her breasts ached.

"We're losing time. Just like on the beach. Remember how much I wanted to make love to you? The whole week I couldn't stop wanting you."

His words made her knees weak and she tried to change the subject. "Even when I was disgustingly sick on the salt water?"

"If you're trying to sidetrack me, it won't work. I've set the stage and now you've got to kiss me if you want to get out of here."

"Fine. One kiss. This is nuts. I told you I don't want to pick up our relationship where it left off because we didn't have a relationship. We had a fling. Why can't a girl have the fling of her dreams and just leave it there? No, it's got to spill over into my life when we both know it won't be the same and can't ever work and—"

He put a finger on her lips. "Shh."

She opened her mouth to bite his finger, but he ran the tip over the curve of her bottom lip.

She raised her face towards him, willing to cooperate, but he didn't do anything else. She felt like such a fool. "Am I supposed to initiate something? Can't we just get this kiss over with?"

"What a thing to say to a Latin man."

"You're mostly American." She put her hand on his chest.

He lowered his head to nuzzle her neck. His chuckle felt warm against her face. "You liked the Latin part. I remember how you melted when I spoke in Spanish."

"You smell good. Like cinnamon," she told him, trying to divert her traitorous thoughts. Yes, she loved it when he spoke Spanish. It made her hot for him. And she was so hot for him now.

"Good. A compliment. I'm already putty in your hands," he teased, rubbing against her.

He was so aroused, it made her ache.

"Can we just get out of here?"

"Then kiss me…"

She captured his jaw with her hand, and with only the slightest hesitation put her lips on his. She waited for him to kiss her back, wanting to keep some kind of emotional distance, not willing to give too much of herself, because to get lost in this fantasy was too dangerous.

He remained stubbornly, maddeningly passive. His lips were full. She loved the texture, soft…and they were trembling. And so was the rest of the warm body pressed against hers. But not with passion.

She jerked away from him. "You're laughing at me!"

She could feel the laughter rolling out of his chest. "Yeah, Emma, I'm laughing. I haven't been kissed like that since Mary-Jane took me to her tree house the summer I turned nine."

She stomped her foot on the floor. "How could you laugh at me? It's humiliating enough that we're in a janitor's closet, after I told you that I don't want to have another office relationship."

"Most women don't mind being waylaid in the closet as long as the guy makes it worthwhile. I've been told that you want to work on a more casual attitude concerning sex and I can help you with that."

"I'll bet."

"Where did Emma go? The girl who wears a thong and gives herself without hesitation? Did you leave that part of you in the tropics? Are you afraid to be that girl?"

She didn't think. She just reacted to the challenge and grabbed his chin, yanking it down to her level. His mouth was already open so she dove into the kiss. sliding her tongue into the cinnamon warmth of his mouth, pressing full length against him, and pushing him backwards into what sounded like a mop and bucket. She ignored it all.

She thrust deeply into his heat, holding on to him, taking him. Trembling herself when she heard him moan.

She showed him no mercy, exploring the hot, wet contours of his mouth.

Andres slid his hands over her bottom and she could feel the material of her skirt bunching above his hands leaving nothing between them.

Sagging against him, Emma was more than willing to allow him a few more liberties, even in the janitor's closet. They bumped against the shelves as they struggled to get closer to one another.

The corner of his mouth fascinated her and she explored it with her tongue. He kneaded her bottom, pulling her closer against the bulge of his erection.

She sighed, burrowing closer still, accidentally knocking into the shelves again, and then something fell down from above them. "Ouch." She reached up to touch the spot where a lightweight box had bounced off her head.

Tony immediately let go of her.

"Tony, I'm all right." She reached out to touch him and found him covered in the slippery material of what felt like trash bags.

"Get them off me," he whispered hoarsely, flinging the bags.

"What? Tony, they're just trash bags."

"I know...but I can't breathe."

He sounded like a little boy, humbled, horrified, and she suddenly realized the problem. "You really are claustrophobic," she said as she helped push the bags off him.

He didn't answer, just kept pushing at the bags.

"Tony! Stop swinging your arms around or you're going to give me a black eye."

Finally, he stopped moving. She heard him take a deep breath. Obviously concentrating.

She leaned in and pressed against him. He wrapped his arms around her as if she were a lifeline and put his head against her shoulder. His large frame shook. She could hear each rasping breath as he held his fear in check.

He's so strong, yet I'm comforting him. Emma blinked back tears. "You shouldn't have brought me in here when you're claustrophobic. What were you thinking?" She scolded.

"About putting my hands on you." He laughed hollowly.

"Can you hang on until I get the lights on?"

"Do you have to go?" He hugged her tightly and then took a deep breath and drew away from her.

She waded through the trash bags and other fallen articles towards the light shining from underneath the door, pushing everything out of her way with her feet until she reached the light switch. "Close your eyes," she warned as she flipped the switch.

He immediately straightened to his full height.

"You don't have to be embarrassed." She leaned against the door, watching him regain his composure. He'd been so vulnerable. And she had to admit how much she still wanted him. But...

He came towards the door, stopping to pick up the mop and gather the bags. He shoved them onto the shelves. "Some seduction. You had to rescue me." He slammed the door behind them and then locked it.

"I've changed my mind," she whispered as they went down the empty hallway. "Maybe…"

"What do you mean?" He stopped to look at her with those fathomless eyes. "I go to pieces and you change your mind?"

She shrugged. "Maybe I've got more to learn. Like how to lighten up and take advantage of being waylaid by handsome men in closets. Maybe you can teach me how to take all of this more casually."

"This doesn't make any sense. I humiliate myself and you want me to waylay you?"

"We can't actually have sex at the office. It's not very professional and I don't think they'd send me to paralegal school if they found out."

He pulled her against him. "Why don't I just take you home with me tonight?"

His offer hit her in the gut. But she took a deep breath and tried to explain. "Because you keep saying how important this is to you. You've rearranged your entire schedule and everything. It's overwhelming. Because I only want the relationship we had on the ship. Fantasy. Foreplay. And…fornication."

That way I won't be devastated when you take off for Denver and never look back.

He ran his fingers over her cheek, looking deeply into her eyes. "Why do you have to be so blunt? You said you wanted to emulate Tina and you've got it down to a science but when are you going to allow yourself just to be Emma? When are you going to trust yourself and what's between the two of us?"

She put her head down. "I can't trust it."

"I'll teach you to trust it."

She shook her head.

He gazed at her thoughtfully for a moment, his brown eyes soft and warm. "But first, *chula,* since you trust the physically intimacy between us, I'll make you my love slave."

"Like on the ship," she breathed. The expectancy was stronger than her fear of getting hurt. "But it's just for fun, until you have to leave."

"I have one stipulation."

His eyes were challenging when she dared to look up at him.

"You have to play your part in this fantasy."

"What?" She moved away from him. This was the reason she couldn't trust him or any man. They always wanted you to change.

He followed her into the employee break room and when the door swung shut behind them he gently pushed her backward until they bumped up against the wall, his body pressed fully against hers. "Your eyes are all hazy and I'm hardly touching you, *chula.*"

"Stop."

He ran his hand up her thigh under her skirt. "I could make you very happy tonight."

"I'd love to. But we've got a deal."

He touched the lace thong between her legs. "Are you sure you don't just want to go straight to the pleasuring?"

He found exactly the right spot under the skirt and petted her, gently, patiently and perfectly.

Emma could feel her defenses cracking wide open. "Don't."

She couldn't finish. His touch was driving her over the edge.

Then the rattle of someone coming down the hall penetrated the haze of desire. She jerked away from him. The sound stopped further up the hallway, then they heard the jingle of keys and finally a door shutting.

Emma let out a moan of relief. She must look a mess with her hair all over the place. She pulled her dress down as far as it would go, tugging and trying to catch her breath. "I don't think this is a good idea after all," she told him.

Her back to him, she continued, "It was a crazy idea. A sexy idea. But I'm not really interested."

"You can't spend your life hiding from the sensual woman you are. What are you running from?"

"Heartache, humiliation," she said flippantly. She walked over to the fridge and opened it. The cool air rushed over her heated flesh, reminding her how the ocean mist had caressed her skin...

He came up behind her. "We have a deal and I'm going to fulfill my part of it."

That voice washed over her like surf in the moonlight, the voice of a man who couldn't exist, a voice out of a dream. "So it's just my sexual response you're interested in? Nothing more. Nothing serious."

Tony didn't know what else to do. He wanted her badly. If he could pleasure her body, and seduce her mind, then perhaps he could eventually reach her heart. "Yes."

"No strings? No expectations between us but a good time?"

"Isn't that the way you want it? Casual sex. No feelings. No strings." He could be blunt, too.

Especially if it shook her out of denial.

She fidgeted. "I guess that's what I want."

"Okay. That's the way it will be." Tony walked away. He couldn't stay any longer without saying what was in his heart.

That he wanted her.

Maybe forever.

10

THE NEXT MORNING Emma lay facedown on the edge of her feather pillow, feeling weak and drained. It was only the middle of the week and already she was exhausted. Maybe she'd call in sick and head for the beach.

She pushed the pink-and-yellow sheets off her heated skin. Was she having hot flashes?

Or was it the residue of another one of those dreams where Andres ravished her body in a variety of ways? She'd never known she could be so imaginative. Those damn dreams haunted her nights, and now it looked as though he intended to haunt her days.

Last night she'd come home so aroused that she should have gotten her battery-operated friend out and taken care of the itch.

But she'd remembered Tina's comment about a man's equipment being better than anything they could buy on the Internet. Emma felt sure the mechanical device would have left her disappointed and unsatisfied after being intimate with Tony.

He can't have ruined me for the Rabbit!

Emma smirked as she climbed out of bed. At least she hadn't lost her sense of humor!

She went into the bathroom and gazed at herself in the mirror. She even looked like a woman who'd been ravished. Her hair was all over the place and her skin flushed with heat.

You just need some time, she told the woman in the mirror.

Perspective.

Things had been going well. She'd felt confident and womanly, except when Lance had put his hand on her derriere.

Maybe the cruise and all its fantasy were still too fresh. But she had to face it, had to live in the real world where a woman shouldn't be fazed when a man made a pass at her.

She unsnarled a strand of her hair and then wrapped it around her fingers. *Today Tony's going to seduce me. And I'll say yes.*

Where had that crazy idea come from? She knew where. Yesterday he'd been weak, frightened and utterly adorable. What could a woman do when a man made a fool of himself just so he could put his hands on her?

Emma washed her hair in the cool spray of the shower, hesitating only a second before she reached for the straightening mousse. So what if he seduced her? she thought as she put the mousse on her hair.

Just think about it as the next step in the plan. Casual sex without the ship.

Practice.

And I won't have to go to bed frustrated. He'll be leaving soon enough and then she'll go back to the Rabbit. Or maybe even Lance.

"THIS IS CRAZY. Old Man Smith won't have any viruses or porn on his computer. Why don't we go back to the system core?" Emma demanded.

Then she glimpsed Tony pulling something out of his bag. "What are those?" Emma looked curiously over the square papers Tony started laying out on the desk in front of her. They were working on the far edge of the work area in Smith's office.

Alone.

"They're fake tattoos. The kind that wear off in a day or so."

"Tattoos?" She hoped she didn't sound too excited. No one knew about her secret preoccupation with tattoos or her lack of gumption to get one.

"Yeah, I thought it might be fun to give you a tattoo. I heard you tell Tina that you wanted one."

She considered the gleam in his eyes and half hoped there was a catch. "That was different. Tina and I agreed that I would get a temporary tattoo to celebrate being liberated from my sexual inhibitions." She'd elaborated on the truth on purpose.

He didn't even blink. "And these will help you let go of any remaining inhibitions, so it kinda fits."

"So you think I have inhibitions after everything we did on the cruise?" She leaned in close.

"If you do, this will certainly take care of them."

Reaching out to touch one of the papers she said, "It sounds interesting, but where did you intend to put that tattoo?"

"On you." He reached out and touched her straightened hair where it brushed her shoulders.

She nodded. "I figured that, but where?"

"Wherever you want it."

Smith's desk was pristine, without even a paperweight to mar the oak surface. Emma had a vision of herself spread out on that desk, dress around her waist and Tony bent over her, penetrating her slowly, so slowly.

She suddenly felt a hot flash coming on.

Tony held one of the tattoos closer, like an offering. Could he sense what she was thinking?

Staring down at the colorful design she wondered why she had denied this part of herself. Hadn't she always wanted a tattoo? She'd even gone into the tattoo parlor down on Eagle Street, and then changed her mind when the guy with multiple lip piercings had asked her what design she wanted. She hadn't been courageous enough to make that dream come true. She hadn't even had the guts to admit it to her best friend because she knew Tina would drag her to the tattoo parlor and it just wasn't the same as having the courage to go herself.

"Choose one," he urged her.

Looking at the toucans, lush flowers entwined with symbols, and a heart that said Bad Girl, she didn't see anything interesting. "There aren't any simple ones?"

"You're not a simple girl."

It made her feel warm all over. And he looked so hot. Today his slacks were gray and his shirt white. It was a gorgeous contrast to his dark skin and his hair, which curled around his ears and over one eye. Today she could definitely see her pirate in the computer geek.

"Where did you get those?"

Tony was obviously multifaceted.

"I got them out of a machine at the arcade."

"This flower looks just like…" She couldn't finish the thought aloud.

"Like labia?"

Emma pulled away from the innocent piece of paper.

"That's because you're thinking about sex. Just as I am."

"How do you know I'm thinking about sex?"

"Because your eyes are hazy."

It probably wouldn't do any good to lie to him. She licked her lips. "You pick one for me." Her voice sounded husky. This child's game was getting to her. He was getting to her.

"Okay, the rose, the one with the dagger."

"Why?"

"Because you're dangerous."

She squared her shoulders—first passionate and now dangerous. With him she felt as though she could be anything.

She watched him reach inside his pants pocket. He held up a handkerchief for inspection. "Nothing dangerous hiding inside there."

She laughed. She couldn't seem to help it.

"Where shall we put the rose?"

Chewing on her bottom lip to keep from laughing out loud, Emma admitted, "I'm not sure. I've never had the courage to get a tattoo before—even a temporary one."

He leaned in close, so close. "No one else will know. It doesn't have to show."

Considering her options, she admitted, "If everyone sees it then I'll have to answer a lot of uncomfortable questions about it. So why do I want a tattoo?" But she did. Just the thought of it made her heart pound.

"Because you're trying new things, walking on the wild side and experimenting. And you don't have to worry, you're safe with me."

"I'm not sure a fake tattoo qualifies as walking on the wild side."

"We can put the tattoo on your shoulder."

"That's not where I would put it if it were an actual tattoo," she blurted without thinking.

"Where would you put it?" He came closer.

If she parted her legs he could move just a step and be between them.

Impulsively, she took the hem of the modest black dress she wore in hand and pulled it up, high enough to reveal the tops of her thigh-high stockings.

"Garters?"

She shook her head. "Elastic."

He looked as if he might drool. "If I put this on the inside of your thigh, is it going to make you feel naughty? Wild? Hot?"

If he put his hand on the inside of her thigh it was going to make her demand he push her up on this desk and pull out that very dangerous weapon in his pants. After all, they had the privacy, and she really, really needed him. "I'll feel more than naughty, knowing I have it there."

He slid his hand up a few inches and she felt every one of those inches to her core. He stopped about a hand's length from her panty edge. "Here?"

She nodded. Unable to speak without begging.

"You'll have to roll down your stocking."

She had to gather her concentration in order to respond to him without drooling or pleading with him to break his promise not to have actual sex with her at the office.

"Is this the right spot?" He sounded too smug. Well, she'd take care of that.

"No, I think it might show in my workout shorts, they're pretty short." She opened her legs and then took his hand and put it nearly to the edge of her thong, on the inside of her thigh. "Better put it here, where no one will see it."

Payback.

But he only smiled. A slow smile, full of desire.

He opened a bottle of water that had been sitting on the desk and wet the handkerchief. Then he pressed the tattoo to her thigh and rubbed it with the cloth, back and forth, with excruciating attention to every bit of the tattoo.

Emma threw back her head. Her loose hair brushed her shoulders sensuously. *Suddenly I'm powerful, wicked and wanton, and all because of Tony*. But who was she kidding? This was just fallout from the cruise. That was why she couldn't stop thinking about him.

"Emma."

His voice was full of need.

Her nipples burned.

"Don't wiggle," he instructed in a husky voice.

His hands shook against her leg.

He dropped the handkerchief and looked at her almost helplessly.

She spread her legs so he could retrieve it.

His warm hands brushed between her legs. She drew

in a sharp deep breath of protest, shifting a little to try to relieve the pressure that was building. He had only to touch her to ease the torture.

Was he as hungry for her as she was for him?

He swallowed audibly, then bent down to continue applying the tattoo.

She thought of all the work on her desk, a hurricane, menstrual cramping, anything to distract herself from the melting pleasure of his intimate, yet thus far, impersonal touch.

When he finally lifted the tattoo paper she felt as if she'd been deflated.

"There. How do you like it?"

She took a quick look, then pushed the dress down over the rose and dagger. "I like it. It makes me want to go and show it off." She curled her hands to keep from reaching for him.

Without warning, he yanked her off the desk and into his arms. His kiss overwhelmed. Deep and primal, he took her mouth. She melted into his embrace.

Just as suddenly he tore away, breathing hard. He paced the length of the office. Once. Twice. He moved beautifully, like a panther.

She grabbed the desk with both hands to keep from falling. The entire time they'd done the tattoo, the office had seemed so intimate, but suddenly it seemed huge and she felt lost inside it.

He approached the desk and she took a deep breath, but he stepped carefully around her and then sat down. He shook his head as though exasperated and then gave a defeated smile. "That will be all, Miss Daniels. Thank you for your expert cooperation in this matter. Would you see yourself out?"

She let go of the desk, outraged. "How dare you treat me like this after everything…" Here she trailed off. It wasn't as though he'd taken advantage of her. Could she be outraged that he hadn't thrown her down on his desk and made passionate love to her? She'd set those stupid rules.

She floundered.

He leaned forward, all mirth gone from his predatory eyes. "I'm trying to control my baser urges because you don't want me to lay you down on this desk and make love to you right now, do you? You made the rules. I will, however, be glad to take you for a late lunch and stop somewhere for a session of lovemaking."

"Don't call it lovemaking. It's sex. Just sex." She pulled on her hair.

He waved a hand in frustration. "I don't know if it's just sex or not, but I'd like a chance to find out. Emma, will you give me that chance?"

"No. This thing between us is supposed to stay casual. That way when you get tired of me I won't get hurt and neither will you." She told him practically, emphatically, determinedly. Hoping he'd argue at least a little.

"Okay I'll play this by your rules. All I know is that I want you."

He hadn't argued. But he looked harried as he ran his hand through his hair, his eyes blazing.

Of course, he couldn't feel anything but desire. He

couldn't possibly care for her. He didn't even know her. The woman on the cruise wasn't the real Emma.

"I want to see you this weekend," he said, his eyes still glittering in a way that almost frightened her.

"I don't know."

His expression didn't change. "This weekend. Even if we only hold hands and walk on the beach."

"I don't know if that's a good idea." She turned and hurried to the door. She paused half in and half out of the door. "Remember, you agreed to my rules."

He rose from behind the desk. "I'm feeling like all bets are off. If I wasn't sure you'd change your mind on the way to my house I'd bundle you up right now and take you home to be ravished."

"That sounds like a threat."

"You can take it as a promise."

She shut the door and scooted down the hall. When it became clear he wasn't following, she slowed her pace. She took a deep breath, let her hips swing a little, not sure if it was the tattoo or the memory of his kiss that made her feel every inch a desirable woman.

Then she realized she'd never asked him what he meant by all bets being off. Did he mean what she thought he meant?

A hand on her arm stopped her in mid-swing.

"Hey, Emma." Lance the office letch smiled at her.

"Hello, Mr. Levine."

"How's the new project going? I hear you're helping Enderlin with the computer work. I didn't know you knew your way around a computer or I would have asked you to help me out a long time ago. I'm afraid I'm terrible at technology."

Lance had his charming face on, as he always did when he tried to pick up women at the office. Which was often. Seemed it was too much trouble to hunt them down in the real world. Still she had to remember that she intended to keep him as a potential practice object for when the thing with Tony cooled down. "The project's going well. Mr. Enderlin is very good at what he does."

"I'll bet he is."

He looked so innocent saying it, but she knew he meant it suggestively.

"You look lovely today."

"Thanks."

He reached out and touched her hair lightly. "I like your hair down. It looks sexy."

She took a step away but he moved with her. It seemed he was on the hunt and she was the quarry. Funny, he'd never been so interested before. Was it the grapevine?

"Would you be interested in having dinner with me Friday night?"

"I'm afraid I have plans for the weekend. I'm going to a friend's beach house." It was an excuse.

"What about lunch? We could get to know each other."

"I've kinda been ordered to help Tony—Mr. Enderlin until he's finished with the project."

Lance gazed into her eyes. "Let me know when you're done with the project or if you change your mind."

Emma just smiled and nodded. On the way down the hall she wondered if she was the gossip of the day but then discovered this time she didn't care. She had more important things to worry about as she headed towards her office to pick up her things before going home.

On the radio in the car, they called it hump day. Wednesday, the middle of the week. Emma just groaned. Did everything have to remind her of sex? She drove home wondering what she was doing headed back to her lonely apartment when she could be getting naughty. Was she crazy or what?

Was Tony headed home alone? And what did his place look like? The company had arranged one of those long-term hotels. Those places could be nice. There was probably a desk they could use to have wild sex on; in fact, they could try out all of the available surfaces.

She wished she could break this habit of holding back at the wrong time. Caution had its place, but its place was definitely behind great sex—several places behind.

"Emma."

"Yeah?" She leaned over to see what Tony was doing on the computer in yet another office, bright and early Thursday morning.

"You do know that we don't have to check every computer on the network, don't you?" His grin made her feel as if they were sharing a secret.

She smiled, a slow seductive smile. "I know."

Today's workday wasn't going to be so innocent because last night she'd gotten thoroughly fed up with frustration. She'd decided sex was a necessity. After all, she'd already had sex with Tony. What was she holding out for?

She was desperately hoping he'd brought the tattoos again today.

"I don't want you to think I'm charging the company for all of this extra time."

"I wouldn't let you."

They worked in silence for a few minutes but she couldn't stand it for long. "Tony?"

"Yeah."

"Did you bring those tattoos?"

"I might have."

"I think I might want another one."

"Really? Which one?"

Rubbing her hands together, she told him, "You'll have to choose. I'm hopeless, no imagination."

He reached into a nylon bag that held his computer stuff. "I think I like the lightning bolt. It's kinda how you hit me sitting there at the desk with that challenging look in your lovely eyes. That look makes me wonder what you're thinking."

The seductive smile curving her mouth felt so natural. "What a sweet thing to say. How about you put the lightning bolt somewhere on my arm," she teased.

He picked up her almost bare arm and ran his hand along it from top to bottom. In a very courtly manner he brought her fingertips to his mouth. Then he kissed her cupped palm.

"I think it will get washed off your hand." He moved on to run the tip of his tongue over the inside of her wrist. "I can feel your pulse here. Maybe I should put the tattoo here on your wrist."

She pulled her arm away. Her heart beat furiously in

her breast. She felt as if she couldn't catch her breath. "It'll come off too soon there, too. I don't think the wrist will do at all."

He put his hands on her shoulders. Gently he massaged her shoulders, round and round until she felt boneless.

"I could put the tattoo on the edge of your shoulder or on your back."

"As good as this little massage feels I don't want the tattoo on my shoulder. In fact, I don't want it on my arm at all. I think I want the tattoo in a much more interesting spot."

"Where?" He sounded decidedly enthusiastic.

She touched her bottom. "A cheek. A cheeky tattoo."

He went completely still. "Where?"

"You heard me."

"You're going to lie on this desk with your panties down so I can apply one of those tattoos to your derriere?"

Put in such a way, it sounded bold, sensual and risky. *And if this doesn't get me his undivided attention then there's no hope, and I'll just resign myself to the Rabbit.* "Actually I'll just lie there in my thong if that's okay."

He stood there for a moment longer. "Are you sure?"

She nodded, knowing she'd beg if she opened her mouth. Surely he wouldn't resist her this time. He'd lay her down and have her.

He went over to the door and locked it. "If anyone tries this door then there's going to be some gossip. Is that okay with you? I don't want you to go through another episode like the one with Brad."

"I could care less what people say." And she actually didn't care. It felt amazing. There would be no hiding out in the break room this time around. "Besides, the gossips already have us banging each other on the desks in each one of the offices."

"What?" Tony asked hoarsely.

"Some people have already made up their minds about what we're doing in all of the different offices. Can't you just see it?" She unbuttoned the top button of her dress. "We get to an office and then I get undressed." She unbuttoned another button.

He didn't say anything; he just watched her avidly.

"Then I unzip your slacks and ease you out of your pants, then you pull me to the edge of the desk. You rub your cock up against me until I finally beg for release and then you pull me closer and plunge into me." She looked over at him to see if she'd had the desired effect on him.

He looked stunned and there was a blush climbing his neck to his face. "Emma."

She sighed. "Well, I have to admit I've been thinking about it. Constantly."

"I thought you didn't want to have sex at the office. You wanted to be a professional and all of that."

"Maybe I'm tired of being a professional. Maybe I want a little more of what we had on the cruise."

He fumbled with the little papers with the tattoos. Then he looked at her. "I'm definitely interested."

"Good." She finished unbuttoning the dress and then laid it behind her on the desk. Her bra and thong set was lace and left almost nothing to the imagination.

"What are you doing? I thought you wanted the tattoo on your…" He gulped. His eyes touched her as if he wanted to grab her.

"You can touch me," she offered.

He shook his head. "Lean over the desk."

"Is this going to be a clinical version of a tattoo? You said you wanted the sensual side of me."

He pointed at the edge of the desk. "Lean over." His voice and hands shook.

A smile bloomed on her face. She leaned over the desk. The edge caught her at thigh level. Her bottom felt every breeze in the room, and she became incredibly aroused.

He could barely keep himself in check at the sight of her sweet, succulent skin.

"Is this all alright?" she asked breathlessly.

She was definitely more than all right. Those curves were spectacular. He wanted to touch her, taste her and so much more.

"Tony, can you see everything? Do you need me to roll one way or the other?"

He knew she was teasing him, but he wasn't sure if he really wanted go through with it. This thing between them was too important to mess up just for physical release. But her casual-sex idea appealed to his baser nature, and that's about when his goal of easing into her confidence and into her life took a back seat to his desire. He looked down at the smooth expanse of skin and her round little ass. Given the amazing temptation she presented, he could hardly be faulted.

"I see you, baby. Just let me get ready."

"I'm so ready for you, Tony."

"I'm not so sure of that. I think we should get together. We can talk tonight."

"We can have sex right now."

"I'm putting on the tattoo," he protested.

"Okay, put it on and then see if you can resist me." Her voice had deepened to a seductive purr which radiated through him.

Tony reminded himself of how adamant she'd been at the beginning of the week about not having sex. He kept telling himself that he didn't want mindless sex, although he knew it wasn't strictly true at this precise moment with her lying open to him.

She put her hand on her left cheek. "I have such an itch here. Can you help me?"

He ran his fingers over the flesh she indicated, where the skin was soft and so incredibly pliant. He could sink into her.

"Thanks. Now here. It's driving me crazy." She began at the side and then ran her fingers over the slope of her buttock to rest between her legs.

"Stop. I'm going to put on this tattoo and you're going to get the hell out of here before we do anything you'll regret."

"Okay. Just relax. I just had this little itch. I don't understand why you're willing to scratch it tonight and not today." Her laugh was husky.

He thought she was blushing. It looked good on her and it reminded him that this sensual creature was Emma who was holding back so much of herself from him. "I think we need to talk and I mean really communicate."

Then he made the ultimate sacrifice and resisted her, applying the cool cloth almost clinically and holding it for the seconds it required.

She squirmed under his hands, which shook clumsily.

It seemed to take forever but finally he could take the cloth away. "Get up. I'm finished."

"No." She stayed put. "Maybe you should do the other cheek."

"Don't push your luck," he growled.

"I want you to touch me. I want you." She sounded so powerful.

"We're not going to do this here."

"I'm lying on this desk in only a bra and thong. Pretend I'm your secretary and you have me as regularly as you have lunch on your desk. Tease me. Push the thong aside and have me."

"I never seduce my secretaries. What kind of a guy do you think I am?"

"The kind who can't resist me. I like it better when you can't resist me, the way you were on our cruise."

She moaned approvingly when his hands settled firmly on the globes of her bottom.

"Tonight I'll knead this firm flesh until you beg." He did and watched as she bit her lip and shuddered under his hands.

"Then I'll drag my hands down and see if you're wet enough to roll over and have my way with." He slid his finger between her thighs and she opened to him.

"Ah, yes. You're hot and wet for me." He stroked her.

She couldn't arch, or lift up, because the desk was hitting her thighs and her legs were hanging off, but the vulnerable position seemed to add to her arousal. "Deeper," she begged.

He stroked deeper.

"Oh, Tony. Roll me over. Touch my breasts and," she begged as his touch deepened, "take me."

He pulled his hands away. A second later he lifted her effortlessly from the edge of the desk and set her on her feet on the floor. Then he looked at her very seriously.

"This can't be what you want. To be taken on a desk like an office floozy." He ran a hand through his hair.

She looked flushed and tousled as if they'd finished what they started. "Don't you want me?" she asked.

His erect penis pushed up the front of his slacks. A fine sheen of perspiration shone on his cheeks. Obviously he did want her.

"Tonight. See me tonight. A regular date where we talk a little, have dinner and then pleasure each other if you're absolutely sure. I'll be happy to prove how much I want you."

"I can't believe you're turning me down."

She crossed her arms over her revealing bra as if she felt vulnerable, and he hoped he might be reaching her.

"I'm sick of our relationship being so impersonal. I want us to connect on levels other than sexual ones."

"This is not possible." She tossed her pretty hair over one shoulder. "I'm being the most seductive woman I know how to be, I'm practically begging you to make love to me, and you want to connect on other levels?"

He hardened his heart. She might feel betrayed. But he also felt that way and he was beginning to wonder if she ever intended to offer him any more of herself.

"The stupid tattoos proved my body is yours for the taking. Now you want something more from me," she complained. "What else can I possibly give you?"

"A little bit of yourself. Emma. Is that so hard?"

"I'm a sophisticated woman who can decide when and where I want sex—"

"This is hardly sophisticated," he commented, though her tantrum was an honest and reassuring show of emotion. "Are you thinking about what you're doing?"

"I don't need to think. Thinking is what got me into the Brad fiasco. I'm just trying to feel. Don't you just want to feel me?" She ran her hands down the sides of her breasts.

Of course he wanted to feel her. Did she think he was made of stone? But he wanted something more. He wanted to break through her stubborn insistence on putting sexual gratification before any emotional connection. "First you seek out a stranger on the cruise. Then when we see each other again you don't want to have sex at the office, but now here we are at the office and you've got an itch you want me to scratch."

"An itch you caused."

"Because I want you any and every way I can get you."

She pulled on her hair. "Well, you can't have me for more than sex."

"That's pretty obvious because we never talk about you even though we've spent hours alone. I have to drag personal information out of you."

"We don't need to exchange personal information. You already know more about me than I ever imagined."

Tony snorted. "We started out this relationship assbackwards but we can change it around."

She resisted the urge to cover herself. She'd never felt so naked in front of him. "I never asked for more than a casual relationship."

"No, no you didn't." He took a step toward the door. "Let yourself out whenever you're dressed."

She noticed how his hungry gaze lingered where her breasts practically overflowed out of the top of her demi bra. He even licked his lips. It took away some of the sting when he turned from her and stalked out of the office, securing the lock before he closed the door.

Emma sagged into the chair. Then she stood up and twisted around to look at the lightning bolt on her bottom.

And he thinks I hit him like a lightning bolt. All he has to do is spend four days with me and I want to throw my professionalism to the wind and have sex with him.

But it was more than that. She didn't want to know how much more. It would likely scare her to death.

She stroked the tattoo. *How do I tell him that I'm the one who's been hit by lightning and I'm terrified of being scorched?*

A FEW MINUTES later Emma settled into her chair at her desk. Almost settled.

Her heart pounded and she was aroused as hell, but the familiar surroundings with all of her pictures and memorabilia soothed her spirit. A picture of her on the cruise ship with Tina caught her attention and she ran a finger over the happy woman with the swinging hair.

Who exactly was Emma Daniels?

Her mother smiled at her from another frame. Emma picked up the picture and examined it lovingly. Her parents had divorced several years ago. It had been a complete shock to both Emma and her mother. Apparently, her father had been bored for most of the years he'd been with them. After twenty-five years, he'd packed up and moved out.

How could a woman keep a man interested? What did it take to make a home and a life that wouldn't fall apart?

Obviously it wasn't sexual fantasy.

After Brad it had seemed safer not to expect anything more than short-term casual sex. She'd tried being practical and then she'd thrown caution to the wind.

How come it had all blown up in her face?

11

WHEN SHE got inside her apartment it seemed emptier than usual; even her anemones and her clown fish seemed lethargic. Emma put a bag of cheese-flavored popcorn in the microwave and then went to change out of her skirt and into her frumpy sweatpants.

As Emma stripped out of her clothes she had to admit the tattoos had fulfilled their purposes. Could anything be sexier than a man putting a tattoo on your body?

Of course, he'd refused to follow through, but she knew Tony well enough to know that he was being a gentleman—although she hadn't seen it that way at the time. In fact she'd been angry because she'd felt vulnerable. But then he'd said he wanted more than her body; he wanted her mind. How could a woman feel rejected under those conditions?

Now in her comfortable clothes, Emma flopped down on her yellow comforter. Tomorrow there needed to be a change of policy. They wouldn't have sex at work until the building was empty—practically empty. And then they'd go to his place and have sex again.

She ran her hand over the comforter. They could come here and have sex. They could use ice cream or whipped cream and whatever else was on hand.

And there was the Lookout. Hadn't she always wanted to try the hangout they called the Lookout? While Tony certainly had the stamina for all of these sexual adventures, there was so little time. He'd be returning to Denver soon.

And she supposed she'd try opening up to him a little, telling him more about herself, but he'd probably never notice for all of the amazing sex. He didn't understand that she was trying to protect her heart and to spare him from having to dump her when he went back home to Colorado. Emma felt her heart sink at the thought of him leaving. She absently rubbed her chest under the T-shirt.

The dinging of the microwave had her trudging into the kitchen to get the popcorn. She put it on the counter to cool, and then grabbed a citrus-flavored water.

A few minutes later she had the snack all set up in front of her TV. All she needed was to put her saddest movie into the DVD player and then she could sob out her frustrations to her heart's content—well, she would sob when the heroine was bravely dying from cancer and the hero made all of her dreams come true.

And if Emma could just dig up the courage she'd had on the Grand Bahama beach. There wouldn't be any frustrations to sob about tomorrow. In fact maybe she'd take a chance and give him the intimacy he seemed to want. Could he be ready for a relationship? Was it possible that in trying *not* to have a relationship she'd actually stumbled into one? Didn't God just love that sort of irony?

Did Tony really desire more than her body? Could he want her heart as well? She was almost afraid to hope she'd finally found "the one" because he was certainly perfect, great at sex, handsome, successful and a gentleman. Was it possible? And didn't she owe it to the new Emma to explore the possibility? She rubbed absently at the ache of hope in her chest while she popped a handful of popcorn in her mouth.

Just then there was a pounding on the door and the bell sounded. Emma shook her head. The only one who knocked and rang the bell at the same time was Tina. In fact, the knocking sounded louder and more insistent than usual. Emma knew she should have checked on her friend today, but she'd been so preoccupied. Tina just hadn't been herself since the cruise.

"Tina, just wait a minute. I'm coming."

The ringing stopped, but whoever it was—presumably Tina—was still tapping impatiently. Not a good sign. Emma sighed as she opened the door. She didn't know if she was up to helping her friend with her problems when she couldn't seem to straighten out her own life.

Tina rushed through the door and Emma almost didn't recognize her friend. This was a Tina she'd never seen before, wearing a pair of non-designer jeans and a ratty T-shirt with Rice University Girls Track blazoned across her chest.

"Tina?"

"I brought dinner and it's heavy, so get out of the way." Tina kicked a pair of ancient sneakers off on the tile in front of the door.

"You don't have to do that." Emma protested both the dinner and the shoes coming off. "I made some popcorn."

"They're ancient shoes. Not telling what's on the

bottom. I brought Chinese from Chang's and ice cream and root beer. You can't be miserable if you've got Chinese and ice cream floats."

"How did you know I was miserable?"

Tina finally looked Emma in the face. Her dark eyes were free of any artifice. "Tony stormed out of the office without opening the door for me. He never does that. The man's a classic gentleman. So I went after him and had a little chat. The man's crazy about you."

"What did you talk about?"

"You, your goals and your motivation. I thought he needed to understand where you were coming from and that you were planning on being my paralegal."

Emma followed Tina into the kitchenette and then sank down onto a barstool when her legs would no longer hold her. "Great. Thank you."

"Well, you meddled in my life and see where it's gotten me!"

"So this is about Tyler, is it? I thought you weren't seeing him again after the cruise."

Tina set the bags on the counter that split Emma's kitchen from the living area. "So tell me about the trouble with Tony today."

Emma didn't want to ponder what Tony must be thinking after Tina's little talk with him, so she concentrated on the delicious smell of the best Chinese in three counties. She grabbed one of the bags and began setting little boxes out on the counter. "What did you get? There must be a dozen boxes here." Her heart started to thud. "Did you invite Tony to dinner? Who else are we expecting?"

"No one. I just couldn't make up my mind."

With a sigh, Emma set down a box marked Steamed Rice. "You must have had a date last night."

"Something like that," Tina finally admitted while she unstacked the takeout and then made a neat little row out of the boxes.

"I guess it went badly?"

Tina stopped the stacking. "Why would you say that? I've brought dinner before. And why was Tony angry? Did you tell him to go to hell?"

"I would never do that. But I've never seen you in anything other than designer clothes and you never have trouble making up your mind."

Tina actually made a sound which could have been a sniff. Emma almost panicked. What would she do if the toughest woman she knew broke down? Somehow the world would never feel safe again.

"I'm fine. I was cleaning and I had a craving for Chinese."

Emma almost let it go. She knew Tina would be able to handle whatever problem came along, but for the first time it felt like Emma might have something to offer her friend, if only a little sympathy and girl talk. For some reason Emma thought that the tough lady lawyer didn't have a lot of chances to be just one of the girls. She'd probably never been the *girl* type.

"You can tell me what's wrong. It'll be confidential and everything. Did Tyler do something awful? He's pretty arrogant. It was probably just a matter of time."

Tina grabbed the homemade vanilla ice cream off the counter and rushed over to the freezer. After taking a second to put it inside, Tina shut the door and looked at Emma. "I let him sleep over."

"What?"

"I let him sleep in my bed overnight." Tina sniffed again.

"Why is that the end of the world?" Emma knew she sounded panicked but this was The Shark on the verge of tears and Emma had no idea what to do.

Tina wiped at her eyes with a napkin from the dispenser on the counter. "Don't look so scared. I never cry and I'm not going to start now over some dumb jock."

"He's a lawyer," Emma corrected wondering if she'd accidentally entered some reality TV show. She'd turned down great sex for cheese popcorn, and Tina had let a gorgeous man spend the night and for some reason that meant she needed to drown her sorrows in Chinese food, go back in time to don her track shirt and talk about dating jocks.

Emma shook her head at the absurdity. She'd been right in the break room. Dating was one of the most difficult activities of their time, fraught with enough danger to make a grown lawyer cry. She lowered her head so Tina wouldn't see her smile.

Tina opened several cupboards and slammed them until she finally found the plates. "Trust me, I know he's a lawyer and not a jock. But he's exactly like the jock jerks in college. And he's a lawyer. Which only makes the spending the night thing worse. He'll never let it go. He'll drag it out every time I try to put the boundaries back in place. It'll be a huge problem." The last cupboard rattled and slammed as she shut it.

Emma nodded even though she didn't have a clue what the huge problem was.

"I just want to pig out. Will you pig out with me?"

With the delicious scent of the food wafting around her kitchen Emma figured even a saint couldn't resist those spring rolls. She mentally adjusted her wardrobe for tomorrow—she'd have to go with something with a little more room. She'd probably gain three pounds tonight. "I was just going to watch a movie. Do you want to watch it with me?"

"Is it sappy? I'm not in the mood for happily ever after. What about naked men and gratuitous violence? So do you have something like that?"

"Did Tyler break it off after he spent the night? What a jerk." Emma ripped the top off a box marked Shrimp Fried Rice with enough force to send a couple of peas tumbling to the floor.

Tina's eyes narrowed. "He didn't break it off. I did."

Emma blinked. "So you're on the verge of tears because you let him get away?"

"Are you wearing those ugly sweatpants because you're expecting Tony to come over and screw you? Or are you wearing them because you've had a fight?"

Emma put the box of rice down on the counter with exaggerated care. "That's a gross thing to say. But I'm actually wearing these ugly sweatpants in the hope that Tony will be overcome with lust and take me to the Lookout. We haven't made it to the ole lovers' hangout yet."

"I'm sorry. Are you trying to misdirect the witness? You're pretty good. Where did you learn your technique? Melissa or some cheesy TV show? Remember, I saw Tony leave the office tonight and he looked hot and bothered."

"This is Florida. Everyone looks hot and bothered."

"I think his fly was undone. Did you have his pants off?"

"I didn't take off his...oh, you don't play fair, counselor." Emma felt herself blush. She reached out and Tina handed her a plate. Emma put at least five kinds of Chinese food on the plate, along with two spring rolls, until it was a very satisfying, heaping helping of food.

Tina opened the large bottle of soda on the counter. "Do you want root beer in a float or on its own?"

Usually sugary drinks weren't appealing. Emma preferred flavored diet water, but maybe Tina was right. Sometimes a girl had to drown her sorrows. "Plain now, and later with ice cream."

For the first time since she'd come to the apartment, Tina smiled.

Emma grinned back. "Although soda is not going to ensure you're forgiven for meddling in my love life."

"You danced with Tyler. This is mostly your fault."

They settled in with their plates on the coffee table. Emma sat on the couch and Tina slid her long, lean legs underneath the table to lean against the couch. Emma turned on the DVD player with the remote. The movie previews started up.

"This movie must be a couple of years old. I don't remember seeing it." Tina remarked around a mouthful of sweet and sour chicken. Then she licked her fingers.

Emma thought it would be funny if Tyler could see

Tina now—she looked like a little girl with her hair and her guard down, despite the manicured talons drenched in scarlet-and-gilt nail polish.

"It's older, and you probably won't like it, but too bad, you got to pick out the dinner."

"Really? What a privilege. I got to spend sixty dollars on the takeout we're scarfing. And I don't get to pick the movie. Sounds like a bad date. I've had a few of those, where he forgot his wallet or his bank's made a mistake and his card isn't actually overextended."

"It isn't that bad."

"Believe me, dating is the kiss of death to a relationship. You're so smart to keep it casual between you and Tony, and I told him so."

"We might make it work." Emma held the remote to her chest as if Tina might wrestle it away from her.

"Not a chance in hell." Tina put the plate on her lap and counted on her fingers. "There's the deceit from the cruise, that's number one. Then there's the fact that you work together and may have to work on another project if his company's got good support and software. Third there's the distance thing—you live half a country apart. And then there's paralegal school. It's a no-deal deal. You're just as likely to fly to the Bahamas on your own wings as make it with Tony. Though he seems a decent enough guy."

Emma tried to breath. "Thanks." Had she just been thinking she might try to have a relationship with Tony? Now she couldn't breathe and absolutely wouldn't need the movie in order to break down. She rubbed her throat where it felt as if her heart was now lodged. "I guess I'll start the movie."

"Okay but tell me why we're watching an old sappy movie?"

"Because I need to cry." Emma hugged one of the couch cushions to her chest. "And I don't want a lot of crap from you."

"What has crying got to do with this ancient movie?"

"This is my cry movie."

"What the hell is a cry movie?"

"It's a tool I use when I feel frustrated and on the verge of tears. I watch the movie and force the tears. That way they don't surprise me at an inconvenient time—like at work or in front of the wrong person." *Or when I see Tony again and realize Tina's right and it's impossible to have anything more than sex with him.*

"Why would you have to cry? Is that, like, an emotional problem?" Tina turned to ask. "I never thought of you as the girly girl who cries when things get tough."

Emma wanted to smother her with the pillow but the opening scene of the movie came on. "Don't knock the cry movie. I learned it from my mama. Her cry movie was *Casablanca* and it always made her feel better."

"I thought you just said it made her cry." Tina sounded honestly baffled.

"Hush. I'll explain it to you someday when you're feeling like a woman and not a lawyer."

"That's mean." But Tina sounded distracted. She was watching the car chase and eating rice noodles.

"Some of us feel stronger dealing with our emotions instead of suppressing them," Emma lied as she snuggled into the couch. She couldn't tell if Tina heard her or not.

The story unfolded and when the eighteen-year-old girl told her hard-won bad-boy boyfriend she was dying from cancer, Emma heard a sound from below her that sounded suspiciously like a sniff.

She ignored it.

In fact it took the scene where the heroine walked down the aisle with her fiancé smiling at her as though they had a lifetime instead of just a few months together for Tina to finally break down.

Tina was sobbing openly when the credits came on.

Emma just handed her the box of tissues.

Then she handed Tina a pillow, which she clutched like a bridal bouquet.

A minute later Tina was resting her forehead against the smooth edge of the coffee table and letting it all out in a storm of weeping. Emma grabbed the watered-down soda off the coffee table and used the glass to hide her smile though her face felt tight from her own tears. She didn't want to ruin a moment of Tina's first experience with a cry movie.

"WHERE HAVE you been? I was worried about you." He looked down at his watch. "It's almost four."

Emma wrapped her arms around herself. "Maybe I had actual work to do. Remember? I do work here." But she'd been thinking about him all day. She was determined to shock him and get everything she wanted in the process. She'd already fulfilled one fantasy today and she felt very powerful.

"We're in the back this time."

Emma followed him. She knew where they were.

And it was very convenient that most of the staff from this side of the office were in court today, all day.

"I wondered if you were afraid to face me today. I'm sorry about yesterday."

"And I'm sorry that Tina waylaid you. What did she say?"

He grinned. "That you are having the sexual time of your life and she's proud of you."

Blushing, Emma shook her head. "She's crazy."

"I don't know what you see in her, but she's obviously a friend to you, so I just listened. I didn't think any of that came from you."

"I didn't tell her anything except that you were hung like a—"

"What?"

She shook her head and laughed. "Not really. Tina had a fight with the lawyer she's been dating and I think she thought she would save me some heartache. She meant well."

"Right."

"Let's get this done and go home. I'm anxious to be alone with you." Emma closed the door behind them. The computer sat on a huge counter with almost no clutter. No personal items were in this room. And since it was Friday, no papers had to be moved out of the way. There was lots of space.

"Do you still feel the way you felt yesterday?"

"About?"

"Sex at the office?"

He shrugged. "If you promise to take me home with you then I guess I could be persuaded."

She walked up to him. He had on a pair of jeans that clung to those narrow hips as though they were holding on for dear life and loving every minute of it. "I could keep that promise."

His T-shirt was soft under her fingertips as she reached out to stroke the material. "You're wearing jeans today. That's so sexy."

"Hey, I didn't have anything else clean. I can't seem to get organized. I spend all of my evenings thinking about you." He looked so sweetly flustered.

"You do?"

"All the time."

"I have these dreams, X-rated dreams." She ran her hands over his chest and down towards his waistband.

He collected himself rather quickly. Maybe it was the mention of those X-rated dreams, but she'd like to think it was her touch that inspired him.

He leaned down to nuzzle her neck. "Let's scoot out of here now and I'll take you anywhere you want to go, *chula*."

"Oh I expect you'll take me somewhere." She nodded towards the flat open space beside the computer. "I want you to take me right there, right now."

Emma pulled her little silk top over her head, baring her naked breasts. She'd worn it with jeans to the office since she'd taken a personal day to take care of something. "I think we started out something like this. Do you remember?"

He appeared to have trouble answering, but Emma thought he might have nodded.

She reached into her pocket and handed him the little

scrap of fabric like the one he'd once taken as a trophy. "There's nothing under these jeans but me."

"Are you sure about this?" He clutched the thong. "I understand the respect you have for your office and your job."

She reached up to play with one of her erect nipples and saw him catch his breath.

"I still respect the office," she told him. "But some-times a girl has to grab the moment. That night on the beach is one of my fondest memories. Not only the pleasure you brought me, but also the memory of the wild woman I became on that beach. Believe me. I'm sick of being cautious, but I'm not stupid. No one is in this side of the building, so we have lots of privacy."

She walked over to the table, bare breasts bobbing, and then sat on the edge of the table, facing him.

"If you can't bring yourself to participate then I'll just have to take care of myself."

"I wouldn't mind seeing that."

Emma grinned. "Seeing this?" She unzipped her jeans and then pushed the denim out of the way so she could put her fingers directly on her yearning flesh. "I'm so wet. I've been wet all day thinking about having you inside of me. I'm probably making a mess of these jeans right now."

"You're killing me," he groaned.

She didn't look up. "I like to be stroked here." She leaned back, stroking herself. "But you know that. Andres knows exactly how to get me hot."

He came to the table.

Emma moved her hands. Hoping he'd touch her.

He grabbed her hand and brought it to his lips, and then with long, slow laps he licked her fingers. "You taste so good. I'm going to have you for dessert. Then I'm going to fuck you so hard."

"Oh." She was suddenly at a loss for words.

When he'd finished licking her, he cupped one large hand over her clitoris and leaned down to suckle her nipple. "You are unbelievably sexy, Emma. Better than anything a guy could merely imagine, better than any fantasy on a beach and better than any woman I've ever had."

"Oh," she repeated stupidly. She couldn't think as he leaned her back and tugged on her nipples, each in turn. His fingers filled the void between her legs and she came so fast and furiously that it hit her like a wave.

He stroked her gently while the wave receded.

"Oh sweetheart, you are so beautifully responsive. I love the wild woman hiding out in your very smart, very professional body. I love bringing out my siren."

He stroked her breasts and then dragged those clever fingers down over her ribs, stomach and down to the silk between her legs.

"No." She pushed his hand away and turned on her side. "I want another tattoo."

"I didn't bring them. Because of what happened yesterday."

He ran his hand over the curve of her hip. "I love your sweet little ass."

"Even it it's a little different today?"

"What? What's different?"

She rolled a little bit, carefully as the spot was still

sore, and wriggled the jeans down out of the way, then pushed the bandage aside.

He looked and reached out as if he would touch it. "You got a tattoo?" He sounded surprised.

"Yep, but not a rose," she explained, afraid he couldn't tell what it was because of the swelling. "An island flower seemed more appropriate as I was trying to recapture those moments with you."

He leaned down and captured her mouth in a fierce pirate's kiss that Emma dove into. He rolled her over on her back as he thrust into her mouth and then nibbled her tenderly. Drawing away, he ran an absent hand through his tousled hair.

"It looks sore," he said hoarsely. "I don't want to hurt you." But he was unzipping his jeans with an urgency she found very stimulating.

Emma could feel the heat building. "It won't hurt." *Not enough to care.* She only wanted him deep inside of her body, taking her to their island again and again.

His pants slid down, followed by dark briefs. Emma reached out to stroke the length of his penis. "I want you so much."

Pulling her jeans the rest of the way off and then securing her at the edge of the counter, he let her caress him for only a minute, before he drew away from her. "I've got to have you, *chula*."

Tony slipped a condom out of his wallet, carelessly tossing the wallet on the floor as he hastened to open the wrapper. Emma had to help him roll it into place as his hands were shaking.

"I feel like an idiot."

"It makes me feel so powerful. I love how much you want me."

"Now sweetheart," he said gruffly. "I've got to have you now."

Emma found she didn't care which language he used as long as he touched her. He angled her knees up and then pulled her towards him at the very edge of the table.

As he stroked her, he said, "You do look like a flower. A very ripe, very ready flower covered with dew."

Emma could only moan.

"You're so ready for me, *chula*."

"Yes, Tony. It seems like it's been so long." She pushed against his fingers as she pleaded for more.

Then he pulled away.

Emma had only a second to be disappointed before he pulled her to him and, planting his feet on the floor, thrust into her, bringing her to the edge.

She grabbed his waist, pushing herself against his length until he stabbed at the very heart of her. She came with a soft cry.

But he didn't stop. He grabbed her hips. Deeper and deeper he penetrated. The wave didn't recede. It built within her.

It was so intense. Too intense.

She wanted to pull away. But she'd never, ever been here before.

And she wanted it. So this time, she reached for it, opening everything.

He pounded into her, until there was nothing between them and the roaring orgasm that overwhelmed them.

EMMA LAY on her side where he'd eased her down on the table. She looked so small and fragile. "Emma, are you okay, honey? I didn't hurt you, did I?" He couldn't help but reach out to stroke the curve of her hip. She was so incredibly beautiful, and he wanted her again.

Lucky for both of them that his body wasn't ready to accommodate them or else they'd never be able to walk out of here.

"Never. You'd never hurt me." She stretched like a sensuous little cat. "Wow. I think that might have been the most intense orgasm I've ever had." She looked dazed.

"I got carried away. Your tattoo? Is it okay?"

"It's sore, but it was worth it. I'll just pop a couple more painkillers and later tonight we stick to a softer spot, like a mattress." She struggled to rise up on the table.

He helped her up, gently. She felt so wonderful in his arms, soft and pliant. "Where do you want to go? Your place or my hotel?"

She looked at him with those sea-blue eyes. "I'd like to see your place." There was a subtle flush on her cheeks.

"Are you embarrassed to ask me to stay at yours?"

"A little I guess."

He kissed her cheek, helped her to climb down from the table and then watched as she picked up her shirt and pulled it on over her head. "I love it when you don't wear a bra. It's an instant turn-on."

"You didn't even notice until I took the shirt off."

"I noticed the minute you walked in here. Your nipples were hard. Trust me. We guys have naked-nipple radar and it's very accurate. Any time you want to turn me on just let me see a little jiggle and you've got me."

"Are you a breast man?" She looked down, almost shyly.

She'd been a wild woman just a minute ago. It was an intriguing contrast. "I'm an Emma man. I'm infatuated with everything about your luscious body."

"I like you, too." This time she managed to look him in the eyes. "You have a very sexy body."

She was wild and shy, practical and impulsive. That was the paradox that was his Emma.

And the tattoo? How could she have known he found tattoos amazingly sexy? Emma was perfect, a nice girl who was wild in the sack and who intuitively understood his fantasies.

Tony pulled his pants up and secured them. Had she done that for him? Had she been inspired by the cruise?

Emma moved across the room to get a brush out of her purse and smoothed out her hair.

He felt a surge of possessiveness. It might be extremely sexist, but it excited him that the island flower would be part of her for the rest of her life. Now if only she would give him a chance to be a part of her for the rest of her life. Could they make it work?

"Tony? You okay?"

Something was holding her back, but he intended to have her. No matter what she needed, he intended to give it to her. Then maybe she'd realize how much he cared.

"I think I'm ready to go now. Was there anything we needed to do on the computer before we go?"

"If there was, I've forgotten what it was." He approached her. She might think that she'd erased any sign of what they'd been doing, but the flush, the heavy-lidded eyes and the distracted air would instantly give her away.

It made him feel proudly possessive. He smiled. He hoped she never realized what a Neanderthal he was.

She grinned at him. "You're too easily distracted. What kind of computer guy forgets to take care of his program?"

"The kind that's seduced by a beautiful, sexy woman."

"I guess I did seduce you." She looked adorably proud of herself. "Why, I'm more like Tina than I thought. Someday I might even become a mankiller just like her. And *I* didn't get caught. I always knew Brad was a loser."

He felt his heart lurch. Suddenly he realized that caring for this woman might be dangerous. He usually escaped his relationships and headed straight for his computer. Role-playing games were safer and you never got your heart crushed when you didn't rescue the princess. You just went on to game forty-nine or two-hundred-and-eighty-six or whatever. He had a feeling Emma wasn't going to let him play that long.

Maybe he should have listened to Tina. He had a feeling he'd be out of the game—soon.

And it didn't bode well for him. He hadn't been hurt badly since high school, because he hadn't found a woman who could compete with his work. It struck him as ironic that he might be on the other end this time— he might be left behind if Emma intended to become a player. The thought actually brought on a physical ache. "Are you sure you want to be together tonight?"

Was he sure he wanted to?

"Why?" Was there a shadow of insecurity in those lovely eyes?

He squashed his own apprehension. He couldn't bring himself to hurt her. And he doubted he could resist her anyway. "I'm just worried about the tattoo hurting you."

He took her to his place and made love to her in his bed. Later Emma went home in her own car without giving him a clue as to how she felt about him. He thought he could use the time and space to think about how he was going to get to know her without chasing her away.

And he *would* figure it out. His siren would someday admit that she belonged to him, gorgeous body *and* soul.

12

EMMA INVITED Tony over on Saturday afternoon. He came, curious about her place. Once there he made himself at home, grabbing a worn photo album he'd noticed on the bookshelf.

Emma stopped short on her way into the living room with soft drinks.

Tony looked up, wondering at the stricken look on her face.

"Tony, put the album down. It's boring to look at other people's pictures."

He clutched the album because she looked as if she might snatch it out of his hands. "What?"

"Put it down."

"I'm just checking it out. You were pretty cute when you were little."

Emma came to stand over him and deposited the drinks on the coffee table.

He was sitting on the floor, leaning comfortably against the couch with the book in his lap and his legs stretched out under her coffee table.

"We *were* the picture-perfect family. But boring."

"Boring? They look like regular pictures to me."

He touched a photo through the protective plastic coating.

"I look gawky."

"But you turned out pretty hot."

She held out her hand. "Give me the album."

"I like this one." He tapped a picture. "This must be your mom. She looks like you."

"My mother will be pleased to hear that you think we're hot." She laughed. "Now that she's single she'd probably enjoy the compliment."

"I didn't say that."

"I'm kidding."

"Why's she single?"

"Because my dad's a jerk and an idiot and he divorced her." Emma shrugged, obviously embarrassed.

"That must be a pain for both of you."

"Yeah, it was great. And I'd really love to talk about it, except I'd rather you take me to the Lookout and make love to me in the back of your car. I've always wanted to do that."

She bent down and sucked on his ear in a way that instantly drove him crazy and was obviously designed to distract him. He had to remind himself that today he wanted more from her than sex. Today, he wanted to establish a connection. He hoped she'd make love to him and not just have sex.

He patted the couch. "Come here and sit. You can talk about it if you want. I have a family, too. And they sure aren't perfect. My sisters are real brats and I have a great-uncle who's in prison."

"That's not funny."

"If you'd let us talk about something meaningful, then you'd know that it's not meant to be funny."

She wrapped her arms around herself. "So the fantasy isn't enough? What about the tattoo? How am I supposed to keep you interested if that's not enough? What's a regular girl supposed to do?" Emma was shocked when the tears came. "And I can't believe I'm crying. That's why I watched that stupid cry movie." She wiped her eyes. "So I wouldn't do this."

Tony climbed to his feet. He didn't have any idea what a cry movie was. In fact he didn't have any idea what the hell she was talking about. "Okay, just forget the family stuff. Can we just talk about us? Just you and me, together?"

"No we cannot talk about us. We should just keep it a fantasy. You're leaving soon. I thought we could have dinner and then maybe go to the Lookout."

"I know I'm supposed to jump at the chance to have sex but what if I want to talk? At least before we have sex?"

Emma sank down next to him, angry at how unreasonable he was being. Wasn't she giving him what he wanted? Why was he pretending he wanted more? Once she dared to dream of a meaningful relationship, he'd start to feel crowded and get the urge to be free. If Tina couldn't hold a man, then Emma had no chance. No chance at all.

She rushed to get the story over with. "My parents got a divorce after twenty-five years and it bothered me a lot. Probably since I was an only child and I was very close to them." She was proud of how matter-of-fact she sounded.

"How are they doing?"

Realizing that she could hardly object to his interest as it was a normal, polite response, she answered, "They're okay. Dad's got a woman living with him and Mom keeps busy." And surprisingly she felt okay. "I think she's happy."

"But you're still angry?"

"Angry?" She put the soda bottle down. "Angry about what?"

"Anger's a natural reaction when people you love do something that hurts."

"I'm not hurting." She hugged her arms around herself.

"I think your parents' situation has a lot to do with why you're holding back."

Emma hunched her shoulders defensively. "My own experiences would be enough."

"Guys. We might be a pain in the ass but we're not all the same as Brad."

She grinned. "That's true." A tiny bit of tension seemed to drain from her as she admitted it. She took in a soothing breath.

"And your parents, they're doing okay."

"When I asked my dad why he divorced my mother, he said a terrible thing." Her voice trembled. *Oh no, where had that come from?*

"What, honey?"

She sniffed. "Nothing. It's not important."

"It feels important."

She shook her head. "No, it's nothing. I'm just a little angry at my father."

"Then I hate him."

She smirked and then got all misty-eyed as she looked into the fierce eyes of her pirate. "Cute."

"I mean it. I'll even kick his ass. Just say the word."

The pain didn't seem so huge with Tony joking about it. "My father said his life was boring. Mom was boring and of course he meant that I was boring as well. Just one mediocre family." She didn't cry. She held it back. Though her father had made a mockery of the life she'd loved.

Tony reached out without hesitation and hugged her. Not a sensual hug, more like a big bear hug, and Emma couldn't help but melt into his arms.

"That was a crappy thing to say and I'm so sorry. But it sounds like an excuse to me, midlife crisis or something, and he blamed everyone else because he didn't have any balls."

"It's okay. I'm figuring it out." She sniffed.

He leaned over and kissed her on the forehead. "I'm counting on you to figure it out."

What was he talking about? "What?"

"Nothing. Let's go and eat, and then we'll check out this point." He ran his fingers over her breast and stopped to circle her nipple. "Unless you want to call for takeout."

It was close, but she resisted him. They had a nice dinner and he didn't try to get any more information out of her, although he asked her about her work at the law firm.

Now they were parked at the point and Emma couldn't help but feel excited. "You know I've always wanted to do this, but somehow I just never have. I guess the right opportunity never presented itself."

He leaned over. "Maybe the right man never presented himself." His kiss was hungry.

She nibbled his mouth as if it was dessert and then when the kiss was over she told him, "There's no right man. It's better to love the man you're with."

"Now you're hurting my male ego."

"In a minute you'll see how much I want you and your ego will be restored." She reached out and put her hand on the inside of his thigh.

He pulled away. "Just a minute. I have an idea."

"What?" Did she sound as frustrated as she felt? They'd been at the Lookout for at least fifteen minutes and so far they'd listened to music and remarked on the incredible view of the ocean from the bluff but Tony hadn't touched her at all. In fact he'd acted strangely.

"I want you to tell me one personal thing about you and then I'll kiss you." He stretched out in the seat, which he'd lowered almost all the way.

He looks too comfortable, like he plans to go to sleep.

In fact he didn't look at all like a man crazy to ravish a woman. "Why in the world would we waste time on something like that when I'm not wearing a bra and I've got on crotchless panties?"

He made a funny sound. "Where did you get the panties?"

"Tina got them for me as a birthday gift."

"I knew Tina was good for something."

"So get over here and strip them off me."

"I would love to."

"Good. Because I really, really want to kiss you. Everywhere."

"And I want to kiss you, too. But I need you to answer a few questions before we make out. It's important to me. Don't worry, I'm not going to let the local makeout place and crotchless panties go to waste. I'll make it up to you."

So far this whole idea was a disaster. "I already told you about the divorce."

"Just one little piece of information, nothing painful."

"Like what?" she asked reluctantly.

"Just another little question."

She nodded, but she knew he was bound to be disappointed as he learned more about her, and her heart ached. He'd walk away once he realized she was just a regular girl.

"What was it like to be an only child?"

"It was okay. I didn't have to share anything with other children and I had my own room. Now kiss me."

"No. I want a true answer."

She sighed, and thought for a moment. Where to start? "Lonely. It was lonely being an only child. I didn't make friends easily because we moved a lot. So I got close to my mother. We did things together. I guess that's why I have Tina. She was also an only child, sort of, and we just give each other what the other one needs." She leaned over closer to him. "Like the panties."

"Good girl." He reached over and kissed the tip of her breast through her shirt.

Then he kneaded her nipple until she gasped.

Then abruptly, he quit.

"Next question."

"Another one? Why don't you just do the other nipple and then I'll touch you? By then we'll have forgotten about this question thing."

"Didn't I make that one worth your while?"

She didn't answer for a minute, but she couldn't deny it. "Yes. Yes you did."

"Okay, so who was your first kiss with and how did it feel?"

She answered quickly this time, wanting to get this trivia game over with. "John Lewis. He wore braces and it felt hard and mushy all at the same time. I threatened to throw up on him if he did it again." She laughed.

"Very well done and I'm relieved you won't be pining for John." Tony reached over and gave her a very thorough, very deep kiss. "My first kiss was with Mary-Jane and eventually she learned to do an excellent job."

"I'll bet you were an excellent teacher."

"I'll bet I was."

He kneaded her nipple in a very satisfactory fashion. She sucked in the breath he'd stolen away.

"Next one. What was your favorite subject in school?"

She shifted in the seat and pulled the miniskirt she'd worn up to the edge of the panties, hoping he would give up this crazy idea.

He reached over and cupped his hand directly over the slit in the panties. "Are you hoping I'll be driven to touch you here?"

"Yes. Please."

"Give me an answer and I'll slide my finger deep inside you, and I'll stroke you until you come apart."

Practically drooling at the thought, she leaned back. "Biology. I liked the biology lab. I really liked to take care of all the reptiles."

"Snakes?" His fingers penetrated her damp flesh.

"Yeah. And…frogs. I once put a frog down my friend Cheryl's back because she called me a nerd."

She was breathing hard as Tony dipped his fingers inside the slit of the panties and stroked her until she moaned. Then he took them away. "I really liked English."

"No, don't stop," she protested weakly. "Why English?"

"I liked the stories, especially the ones that ended happily ever after." He put his fingers back into the warm, wet flesh he'd been stroking. "Okay. I'm breaking my rule because you're too hard to resist and I want to see those beautiful eyes go all hazy." He teased her damp flesh until she came a few blissful minutes later.

When Emma could think coherently, she noticed with satisfaction that he was leaning in closer to her side of the car and had a glazed look in his eyes. Probably the same look she had in her eyes. *This question thing won't be going on for much longer*.

Instead they'd be steaming up the windows in his rental car.

"Okay, next question." He sounded almost cheerful but Emma could hear the strain in his voice. He had the same effect on her that she had on him.

"What's the most important thing you've ever accomplished?"

Emma's heart sank. Didn't he mean the most exciting? Her small accomplishments wouldn't impress anyone, especially a man who created computer programs and could pretty much write his own contract.

Emma unbuttoned her top all the way. Then she teased her naked, erect nipples. "Aren't you tired of this game? Why don't we play a new game? We can pretend we're in high school and you really want to get in my pants and I really want your high-school ring. We can exchange all kinds of sexual favors."

"Emma—" He sounded a little frustrated. "I want to know more about you than just your beautiful body."

That took a little of the sting out of his statement. "Fine, then tell me the most important thing you've ever done."

"I saved one of my sisters from drowning. I was about sixteen and we were all in the creek and she got in a deep spot, got snagged by a submerged log, and couldn't get out..."

Emma pulled her shirt together as she listened to him continue to describe what happened.

"...and then I got her on the bank, she started coughing, and she was fine. It scared me to death but I started treating my sisters better after that day. I think it was because for the first time I realized they wouldn't necessarily be with me forever. It was quite a shock."

Emma sighed. Her story wasn't nearly as exciting. "I once helped my friend raise money for a playroom in the Emmerson Valley Hospital. Her little cousin spent a lot of time there and she said there weren't any good toys. Anyway, I spent a few months volunteering over there and I learned a lot from those chronically sick kids."

He reached over and stroked her face. "You're such a sweet woman." He bent his head. "You even taste sweet." He fastened his mouth on her nipple and suckled her until the ache was intensely sweet.

And she told him things.

In fact, she told him everything. He asked about her

first pet, and she told him she was allergic to cats. It turned out he was allergic, too. He loved big dogs but he'd never had time for one. He wanted kids and he wanted to teach them to speak Spanish. Emma thought she might like at least two kids but was a little daunted by the thought of little boys since she had a ton of obnoxious boy cousins.

The radio played and they listened comfortably now and again. He wanted to know her favorite kind of music, and when she breathlessly admitted that she thought country music was romantic he rewarded her hugely. The windows were now completely steamed in the car and he changed the station to one playing an old song by the Eagles. They both wanted to travel more extensively. And he took her places she'd never been before. Each detail for a nibble, a kiss, a stroke, until it wasn't difficult to share any of it because he had her so aroused she would have done anything.

And then he pulled her onto his lap in the back seat and she finally had *her* way with him.

IT WAS turning out to be a typical Monday morning. Emma's hair curled all over her head like a frizzy tornado because she'd forgotten to use the mousse when she'd been in the shower. She'd been fantasizing about getting soaped up and then pushed against the tile wall by Tony.

She hadn't been able to get him to stay with her last night and daydreaming in the shower had only made her late and horny, so that she'd absentmindedly put a fingernail through her only pair of stockings, and then decided to go without. While French-braiding, she couldn't get the part right, though braiding had always been easy for her before.

Frizzy and finally in her Honda, she'd noticed she desperately needed gas. Now as she filled the tank, her cell phone rang, and it took her so long to find the stupid thing, she missed the call and had to call Tina back while balancing the gas hose and her cappuccino and the credit card all at the same time.

"Tina? What did you say?" The gas hose had a kink in it, and it seemed to resist Emma's efforts to try and get it into the opening of her tank.

"I had a huge fight with Tyler." Tina sounded awful.

Emma finally got the gas flowing and she propped the phone more securely between her shoulder and her ear as she sipped her coffee. "Why? I thought you broke up with him? Are you back together?"

"He's a lawyer. I told you that I never date lawyers."

"Of course he's a lawyer. You knew he was a lawyer."

The gas total made Emma moan as she grabbed the receipt. She stuffed the little piece of paper in her bra and tried to put the hose away. The hose twisted towards her and she jumped back to avoid getting gas on her tan suede skirt, which she'd worn to impress Tony. "Just a second. I'm trying to get gas."

"He's attempting to ruin my life with his incessant and ridiculous demands. Why would he think that he's more than just a cock to me? Have I given him any encouragement at all?"

"You let him spend the night," Emma pointed out.

"Whose side are you on? The prosecution's? I

thought you were supposed to be a friend, a real girl-friend. You even put me through that cry movie."

"I'm just trying to…" The coffee seemed to jump right out of her hands and it hit the ground with a huge splash that went all over Emma's skirt. "Shit!" She stomped her heel on the asphalt. "Shit, shit, shit."

The voice on the other end rose to an almost frantic volume.

"No," Emma tried to soothe Tina, feeling anything but soothed herself. "I'm not talking to you. I just dropped cappuccino all over my skirt. The gas hose is possessed and you're crying. You never cry. I can't imagine what he did to hurt you, but I'm going to carve him into little pieces."

"All he wants to do is examine every little thing. He wants to reach into my past. What the hell does he think he's doing in my past?" Tina complained. "I never invited him into my pain, and I don't have any pain anyway. No pain."

"Mmm." Emma made soothing sounds. "It sounds totally unreasonable to me."

"Talking, that's always the kiss of death for a rela-tionship built on sex. Doesn't he get that?"

Haven't I said the very same thing about my relation-ship? And didn't I have verbal diarrhea last night? Not that I wasn't thoroughly provoked.

Tina's tirade went on.

Emma managed to tame the gas hose and then strug-gle into her car with everything but the desperately needed caffeine. She even merged into traffic without mishap. "You're right. Men are never satisfied."

"Isn't Tony satisfied with the hot sex?" Tina asked.

"Well, of course he is. We just did it at the Lookout and he was very happy."

"See, Tony's great. And he's leaving. It's the perfect romance. A guy who has a cock and only wants to use it."

"Well." Emma eased out into a congested lane of traffic. "Not really."

But Tina wasn't listening. In fact she went on to tell Emma that she was taking a personal day.

"You're taking a day off?" Emma's voice rose. "You never take a day off."

As Tina rambled on, Emma was still trying to assimilate that Tina was actually too upset to come to work.

"Of course I'll help Rose reschedule your client appointments for today. But I don't think…"

Then Tina said something even more shocking.

"You might even consider a change of scenery? California? Long-term?"

Emma felt numb when she got off the phone. Tina could handle anything. So why was she going off the deep end?

The lawyer had apparently wanted a relationship based on emotional commitment. What the hell did that mean anyway? Sex was a commitment and Tina was probably damn good at sex, just as she was at everything else. In fact Emma herself had become damn good at sex. She'd become just like Tina.

But even Tina had now been hurt. In fact, her best friend sounded seriously rattled. And it wasn't a sappy movie and nerves this time. She'd been crying at the end of that phone call. Seriously sobbing. She even decided not to come to the office. The world just couldn't be right if someone as strong as Tina could be hurt.

Emma thought about how Tony had suddenly started wanting her to talk to him. Oh, he'd make it worth it, he'd said. And then he'd driven her crazy with foreplay until she would have told him anything.

And she had.

What would he say this morning? Did he still think she was a sexy siren? Did he still want to have her on the desk in the computer room? Or was he tired of her? Had all the details of her regular life bored him to death and the fantasy was finally over?

She sighed. What did it matter? It was going to end either way when he finished the project.

But she didn't want it to end, she admitted to herself. She wanted the L-word. She wanted him to love her for all of her emotional baggage and the sexy siren ways he brought out in her. He'd given her so much more than just a voyage of sexual discovery. He'd given her validation in every way. And he kept telling her that he wanted more. But he'd never used the L-word. Did she have the courage to tell him how she felt? That she actually loved him?

Probably not.

Emma didn't know if her tears were for Tina or herself. She speed-dialed Tony. "Tony?" she gulped.

She listened to his response. He sounded…fine.

"Yeah, I'm on my way. I just wanted to see how you were this morning." *Are you bored to death with me? Do you have any revelations you'd like to share?*

"I loved talking to you last night. I felt like we really *connected,*" he teased.

"You liked our conversation?" That felt promising. And she'd liked the connecting part herself. In fact she'd been deliciously sore when she'd gotten up this morning.

"Why are you calling? Did you miss me, sweetheart?"

"Yes, of course. But Tina just called me. And she broke it off with Tyler and she was…upset." *Hysterical, rattled and most likely heartbroken.*

"I'm not surprised. They don't call her The Shark for nothing. That woman has a serious problem. She'll never be able to commit. What animal is it that eats her mate when she's through with him? The praying mantis? That should be her new nickname. I don't envy the poor sap that falls in love with The Praying Mantis."

"I don't think it's because she couldn't commit. What a thing to say. Tina would never eat her mate. What kind of excuse is that? It's usually the man who can't commit." *You could prove that you're different.*

Emma jammed the phone back under her chin as it slipped. "What did you say?"

"She's probably brought this on herself with her bad-ass attitude, which, by the way, probably hides a ton of insecurities."

"What do you mean she brought it on herself? Tina doesn't have any more insecurities than the next person and she has good reason for them. I thought you liked Tina." Emma was breathing hard and she hoped Tony couldn't tell she was hyperventilating.

"I do actually. I just like you better. You're stronger and more womanly than she is."

"I'm stronger than Tina? Are you crazy?" Her voice rose. She almost rammed the car slowing down in front of her, despite its flashing right-turn signal. How was she supposed to think at a time like this?

"Last night we finally connected in every way. It was amazing. I felt as if I'd finally gotten all the way inside you, *chula.*"

Arrogant. How could he be so arrogant? He made Tyler look like a saint, calling her girlfriend insecure, bragging on his technique. "I never let you inside of me in every way! You blackmailed me! With every stroke of your clever fingers you manipulated me!"

"Emma, we're just working around what is left of your insecurities."

"Insecurities? What insecurities?"

"I was just thinking that thing with Brad shook you up."

"Brad! Don't you dare bring him into this!" Did Tony have to make her sound so pathetic? Wasn't that why she'd let go of her inhibitions? So she'd never be pathetic again? So she'd always be in charge and strong? And now the man she loved thought she was insecure.

Emma slammed on the brakes with extra force and then thanked God that she didn't have a coffee cup in her lap as the car lurched to a stop. She said through her teeth, "I think the parameters of our relationship were pretty clear and designed to guard against this very thing. And I'm not insecure! At least *I* don't need to have a relationship just because we've explored some sexual territory."

"How do you make these leaps of logic?" he asked sounding honestly baffled.

And why can't you just say that you love me?

She missed his next words. "What? I'm sorry, there was someone beeping in."

Probably Tina. *Remember, she told herself, if Tina can't handle this, you don't have a prayer.*

Time to get back on a more impersonal track, one where she could forget she wanted more. "I'm kinda emotional right now, Tina and traffic and all, so I'll catch you in a few minutes at the office."

"Okay, we'll talk when you get here. We actually have a lot to discuss because I've got to turn in my travel itinerary today."

"When are you leaving for Denver?" Her stomach plummeted.

"It doesn't have to be over just because I have to get back to Denver, does it?"

"Well, no. I mean that's good. I don't want it to be over. But we still have a little more time, don't we?" Her heart seemed to falter.

"My boss has a little problem and he wants me back."

"You can't be serious."

"We can talk about this."

"Goodbye," she said absently.

Emma slammed down the lid to her phone. "This is crazy!" She took the steering wheel in both hands and drove the rest of the way to work with tears threatening.

The traffic lightened up and so did Emma's distress. However, where she'd earlier been in a terrible hurry to see Tony, now she just couldn't seem to drag herself into the office where she knew he'd be.

She cleaned her skirt, smoothed down her springy hair, and got a fresh cup of coffee before approaching Tony.

Tony was packing his little computer bag.

"Hey, I'm sorry I missed whatever you just finished

working on. I've been running late all morning." She put
a hand up to her hair but didn't dare to touch it as it
might spring up like a halo at any provocation.

He looked up. "It's okay. It was nothing important."

"And I'm sorry I went nuts on the phone this
morning. I just wanted to clarify things between us.
Clear the air."

"You made things very clear. Apparently you didn't
like sharing last night—I manipulated you. And you're
obviously not interested in a relationship at this time so
I just have to respect your decision."

She nodded. Was that what he heard? All he understood?

He just kept fussing with his stuff.

When she could no longer stand the silence she tried
reasoning with him. "You want me to make myself vulnerable to you, more vulnerable than I already have, and
I just can't."

He didn't answer.

Yearning to hear him say something, she toyed with
her hair, feeling vulnerable and confused. How could
Tony expect her to give him everything when he wasn't
willing to say what she needed to hear?

She'd been the one challenged and changed since she
met him. And he had no idea how hard it had been to
be with him on the beach and in all of the places they'd
explored. He'd brought a part of her to life she hadn't
expected, hadn't dreamed of, but still, she couldn't go
all the way and say the words. Not with Tina freaking
out. Not when Emma had made bad choices before.
Had she come all this way only to fail? It appeared that

she had. But there was one thing that always seemed to work. One last thing.

Leaning against the desk in a sexy pose, she teased him. "Since you're finished would you like to examine my tattoo?" She lifted the edge of her skirt to show him that she was completely bare.

He took a step back from the desk. Her stomach immediately knotted up.

"I'm not sure it's a good idea to come to the office half-naked. You're bound to give people the wrong impression." His voice sounded stilted, as if he was acting.

She tried a flirtatious smile. "The skirt is just as conservative as usual. You're the only one who knows there's nothing under it."

Surely he was just playing another game, acting out another fantasy. Was he pretending to be a shocked co-worker who couldn't resist the sexual siren of the office?

She put her coffee cup down on the desk. "Am I giving you the wrong impression?" Running her hands up and down her thighs made her so hot for him.

"Emma, I don't think you understand what you want or what impression you're making."

"A sexy impression, I hope. And I do know what I want. I want to make you crazy for me." Emma slid her fingers up inside the skirt to stroke herself. "Let's pretend you're my boss and I've been resisting you, but today I've finally given up, and I just want you to lay me on your big desk. What do you think?"

Tony watched avidly as she stroked the soft hair between her legs. "I can't think."

"This would feel so much better if you would do it

for me," she whispered. "What can I do to make the fantasy work for you? Get up on the desk with my legs open? Do you want me to straddle you in the chair? You can pretend you're closing a million-dollar deal and I'm rewarding you."

"I want something else altogether." His tone sounded so serious.

Emma could hardly keep track of her scattered thoughts; she was so hot at the thought of him touching her, taking her. But he was still just standing there when she needed him so badly. "Tell me, Tony. I only want to make you as happy as you make me."

"Okay, Emma. I want you to stop trying to distract me and listen to me."

She left the skirt hiked up. "You don't want to have sex?" She reached for him, wanting to stroke him through his pants, needing to feel him. Knowing she could make him want her. "Are you sure you don't want to have sex?"

He caught her hand and gripped it. "No, actually I just want to make love from now on."

She pretended she wasn't impressed. "I don't care what you call it, sweetheart. I just want you to play with me."

His grip tightened just a little bit. "I'm done playing games for the moment. I need you to get serious. I want to know that I mean more to you than just a series of sexual encounters. I want you to come to Denver and see my home, meet my family. I want to be a normal couple that share their emotional baggage."

The L-word was conspicuously lacking, which meant that Tony wasn't as sure as he appeared to be, which meant that her heart was still in jeopardy, which meant she couldn't afford to trust him.

Emma jerked her hand from his and then pulled her skirt down, covering all of her vulnerability. "I can't believe I'm hearing this. All my dating life I've been hearing men complain about the emotional baggage they hear from women. And you're complaining that I haven't unloaded mine?" Her voice rose and she pulled on her French braid. "Why?"

He rubbed his hand over his face. "I know it sounds crazy. But I want more from you."

Hope bloomed in her stomach.

"And?"

"And I want to see you and talk to you on the phone and do all of the things people do."

Hmm. Kind of ambiguous.

She waved a hand impatiently. "Look, if I'm not good enough for you, it's better I find out now. I'm not interested in being hurt again."

"I want you to feel safe with me. I want to know everything about you. I want to share our memories of our childhood and corny stuff like that." Tony sounded as frustrated as she felt.

"You hardly sound sure. Don't you ever worry about being vulnerable?"

Did those eyes flicker? "I'm just saying that we should try it and see what happens," he protested.

She shook her head, unwilling to give him anything he might throw back in her face. "We've got such a good thing going. I don't understand why you want to mess it up."

She needed him. But she couldn't afford to need him. Patting her hair to tame it, she tried to think.

"I feel like I'm a tool you're using to explore your sexuality, not a man you want to be with."

Emma could feel her eyes go wide. "Did Tina tell you that?"

"She told me plenty of stuff. But I figured that out on my own."

"She's just practical. And I'm just being practical. She'd be telling us just to enjoy each other until you leave."

But today Tina fell apart and it was over a man.

He shook his head so decisively it made her dizzy, and a bit sick.

"I can't afford to get in any deeper. I have real feelings for you. I'm leaving for home today. We both know that all the real work on the project was done days ago. I'm no longer sure what I'm doing here."

"Thank you." She crossed her arms to cover the ache in her chest. "What a lovely compliment. I'm so flattered that you enjoyed our sexual encounters."

"Oh, I enjoyed them. I enjoyed the hell out of them. I'll never forget you, Emma. But I just can't take it any further with a woman who only wants to play sex games. Even one as incredible as you."

As he turned to walk away, Emma couldn't help but laugh through her tears at the irony of their role reversal. She'd said the same thing to a couple of guys in her time, and when she'd finally let go of her inhibitions, grown into the person she'd always wanted to be, the guy went and changed all of the rules.

Why did her stomach hurt anyway, when she'd

finally accomplished everything she'd ever dreamed of and she'd let go of everything holding her back? Except maybe that one final inhibition that could have changed everything.

That one scary word.

Love.

13

EMMA DESPERATELY NEEDED something. The weekend loomed and it had been such an empty, lonely week without Tony or Tina. She thought she might try someone close at hand to distract her. Lance the letch was hovering like a vulture. Emma smiled encouragingly at the carelessly handsome lawyer, hoping at the same time he realized she wouldn't sleep with him. She just wanted someone to talk to and maybe to tease a little, to discover if perhaps one day she could share her new sexuality with another guy.

Fat chance, when Tony's all you can think about.

"I guess the thing between you and Tony's all over with."

Lance leaned over her shoulder as she sorted legal briefs on top of the counter. The cologne he wore was heady and expensive, but it didn't move her. She sniffed. "There was never anything between Mr. Enderlin and me."

"Really?" Lance put his hands on either side of her arms, disturbingly close to the sides of her breasts, trapping her against the counter.

"Really." She tried to take a step back but he didn't move. Instead she was pressed closer to him and he was obviously aroused.

"I heard you were giving him head in all of those

car and drive all night if I even spoke to you. But I was trying to figure out why I felt this way. What had gone wrong?" He put his head down.

"It's okay." She patted his arm.

"No it wasn't okay. I'd spent years rescuing the princess and somehow this player messed up the most important game of his life."

"You thought *you* messed up?" She leaned in and rested her face on his neck where she could breathe him in.

"Yes. Because in my way I was just as scared as you, and I have less reason. You had the divorce of your parents and your deranged best friend to influence you—"

"Tina is not deranged. She's…just different," Emma objected. "And she taught me a lot about confidence and sensuality."

"So, I'll kiss her feet later. But for now will you just listen to me? Please?"

Emma pulled on her hair. "I thought you wanted me to talk to you."

He took her head between his hands. He smelled like the cinnamon gum he liked. His eyes were intense. "I'm trying to say that I didn't have any excuse for my fear, except that I've never felt this way before."

"What are you saying? That you forgot to tell me you're scared of having a relationship?"

He put his arms around her and squeezed her as if he thought she might disappear at any moment. "I'm trying to say that I love you. If I can get you to shut up long enough to pay attention." He didn't give her a chance to respond, but rushed on, "I never told you. It didn't even occur to me until this morning. And then I could have kicked myself. How could I have been such an idiot, and will you forgive me?"

Even though he was squeezing the air out of her, for the first time in a long time Emma felt as if she could breathe.

"I'll give you as long as you need to get used to the idea, as long as we can talk at least as often as we make love, because I want all of you, both the regular girl and the sensual siren. I've been in love with you since our first conversation on the phone. That siren voice snared me and never really let me go. So I sailed the sea, tied you up and swept you away. I figure I'll be the luckiest man in the world if my Emma lets me keep her as my pirate's booty for the rest of our lives. I meant to make you my prisoner but instead you've captured me, heart and soul."

The warmth of his love spread through her and it occurred to her that she might never get a word in edgewise.

Then he stopped talking and asked, "Emma? Will you please say something? Or am I going to have to seduce it out of you?"

Not this time. This time she was finally ready to open up.

So the regular girl took a deep breath, smiled, and then let go of everything, but hope for the future. "I love you, too."

* * * * *

*Emma's settled, but Tina is still
on the prowl...for now.
Don't miss seeing Tina meet her
match in January 2007.*

Page-turning drama…

Exotic, glamorous locations…

Intense emotion and passionate seduction…

Sheikhs, princes and billionaire tycoons…

This summer, may we suggest:

THE SHEIKH'S DISOBEDIENT BRIDE
by Jane Porter

On sale June.

AT THE GREEK TYCOON'S BIDDING
by Cathy Williams

On sale July.

THE ITALIAN MILLIONAIRE'S VIRGIN WIFE

On sale August.

With new titles to choose from every month,
discover a world of romance in our books written
by internationally bestselling authors.

HARLEQUIN® *Presents*

It's the ultimate in quality romance!

Available wherever Harlequin books are sold.

www.eHarlequin.com

HPGEN06

Four sisters.
A family legacy.
And someone is out to destroy it.

A captivating new limited continuity, launching June 2006

The most beautiful hotel in New Orleans,
and someone is out to destroy it. But mystery,
danger and some surprising family revelations
and discoveries won't stop the Marchand sisters
from protecting their birthright...
and finding love along the way.

SPECIAL PRICE!

This riveting new saga begins with

In the Dark

by national bestselling author

JUDITH ARNOLD

The party at Hotel Marchand is in full swing when the lights suddenly go out. What does head of security Mac Jensen do first? He's torn between two jobs—protecting the guests at the hotel and keeping the woman he loves safe.

A woman to protect. A hotel to secure. And no idea who's determined to harm them.

On Sale June 2006